Yesterday's Dead

YESTERDAY'S DEAD

PAT BOURKE

Second Story Press

Library and Archives Canada Cataloguing in Publication

Bourke, Pat, 1955-
Yesterday's dead / Pat Bourke.

Issued also in electronic format.
ISBN 978-1-926920-32-0

I. Title.

PS8603.O953Y43 2012 jC813'.6 C2011-908655-7

Third printing 2013

Edited by Jonathan Schmidt
Copyedited by Uma Subramanian
Designed by Melissa Kaita

Printed and bound in Canada

Second Story Press gratefully acknowledges the support of the Ontario Arts Council and the Canada Council for the Arts for our publishing program. We acknowledge the financial support of the Government of Canada through the Canada Book Fund.

ONTARIO ARTS COUNCIL
CONSEIL DES ARTS DE L'ONTARIO
50 YEARS OF ONTARIO GOVERNMENT SUPPORT OF THE ARTS
50 ANS DE SOUTIEN DU GOUVERNEMENT DE L'ONTARIO AUX ARTS

Canada Council for the Arts
Conseil des Arts du Canada

Published by
SECOND STORY PRESS
20 Maud Street, Suite 401
Toronto, ON M5V 2M5
www.secondstorypress.ca

To Barry, who makes all things possible

CHAPTER 1

Meredith half walked, half ran along the wide hallway of Union Station. Her heavy bag banged against her leg as she struggled to keep up with the woman striding briskly toward a stairway.

"Quickly, Margaret. The car is waiting." Mrs. Stinson's sharp words cut through the bustle of the busy railway station. "And for heaven's sake, make yourself presentable!"

Meredith's face went hot. She wished she'd washed her face before the train pulled in. She could still taste the peppermint stick Mama had tucked into her pocket just before she'd boarded the train for the long trip to Toronto.

"Remember," Mama had said, "you can always come home. We'll manage." Meredith's younger sister, Ellen, had thrown her arms around Meredith's neck and cried.

Meredith dug in the pocket of her coat, fished out her hanky and scrubbed at the corners of her mouth. She didn't regret that peppermint stick one bit.

Mrs. Stinson's polished shoes clicked up the stairs so fast that Meredith had to scramble. Her arm ached from lugging her suitcase. Its sides strained against the twine Mama had tied around it when they'd finished packing the night before.

"There," Mama had said, "that should keep all your things safe until you need them."

All her things. Meredith blinked away the memory of Mama and Ellen at home in Port Stuart.

Halfway up the staircase, Meredith set the bag down to rest her arm, but Mrs. Stinson had already reached the top and disappeared from view. Meredith heaved the bag off the step, but the handle slipped out of her sweaty fingers.

"Look out!" she cried. Two startled soldiers jumped aside as the battered bag bounced past. It hit the center railing, then tumbled end-over-end down the stairs, narrowly missing a small dog being coaxed up by an elegantly dressed woman and flying past an elderly porter who nearly lost his footing.

The twine snapped as the bag thumped onto the floor and popped open. Out spewed Meredith's possessions into the trampling paths of travelers—her nightgown, everyday dresses, blouses and skirts, the two sweaters Mama had knit, her Bible, three pairs of woolen stockings, writing paper, the pencils from Aunt Jane, a washcloth and towel and precious bar of soap, and, mortifyingly, all her underthings.

One stocking lay marooned against a shoeshine stand. The shoeshine boy was grinning. The little dog was barking. The soldiers were laughing.

Meredith's face burned for the second time since the train had pulled in.

"Margaret?" Mrs. Stinson called, sharp as ice. "For heaven's sake, come along!" She stood at the top of the steps, shaking her head at the exploded suitcase.

"I'm sorry," Meredith said. "I lost my grip."

"How very careless." Mrs. Stinson frowned as she surveyed the mess.

Meredith hurried down the stairs. She plucked her belongings from the floor and stuffed them into the suitcase. The catch wouldn't close, so she scooped the awkward bundle into her arms and started up the stairs.

"I am not convinced you will suit the Waterton family, Margaret," Mrs. Stinson said. "We shall have to see."

Meredith forgot her embarrassment. She'd never have dropped the suitcase if she hadn't had to sprint after Mrs. Stinson. She pulled herself up to her full height and glared at Mrs. Stinson, her scowl reflected in the woman's shiny black patent purse.

"It's *Meredith*," she said. "Meredith Hollings." She met Mrs. Stinson's cool gaze square-on.

"You need to learn to curb your tongue," Mrs. Stinson snapped. Her eyes traveled over the hat that had been Mama's, the too-small coat and the scuffed brown leather of Meredith's school shoes. "What a lot of fuss over a name. Follow me, and for heaven's sake, don't dawdle."

Mrs. Stinson turned abruptly and marched toward a set of tall brass doors.

I *will* suit the Watertons, Meredith vowed as she followed Mrs. Stinson through the soaring hall of the train station. I have to.

CHAPTER 2

The October afternoon was bright after the dimly lit station hall. As the brass doors swung shut behind her, Meredith peered up the street, looking for Mrs. Stinson. Smartly dressed women, their hats like bright birds, bunched in front of the shop windows lining the street. Colorful signs jutted over the sidewalk from tall brick buildings. Men in dark suits, hats firmly on their heads, strode past.

"Latest news from the Front! Spanish Flu in Niagara Camp!" A small man waved a newspaper in Meredith's face. "*Toronto Daily Star*! Two cents! All the news! Right here!"

The creaking of a delivery cart and the clopping of its tired-looking horse reminded Meredith of home, but the busy, beeping automobiles speeding past told her she was in Toronto. She'd never seen so many automobiles in one place.

"Over here, girl!" Mrs. Stinson called from the long line of black automobiles parked in front of the station. "You mustn't lollygag. Dr. Waterton is expecting us."

Meredith hugged her load to her chest—she didn't want to spill her suitcase here, too—and started toward the waiting car.

"Miss?"

It was the boy who had grinned at her inside the station. The curly, red hair under his cap was the same color as the freckles that covered his face, but Meredith's gaze was fixed on the long woolen stocking dangling from his fist.

"I think this is yours?" he said.

Meredith felt her face go hot all over again as he dropped her stocking onto the jumble in her arms. She glanced toward the waiting car. Mrs. Stinson was frowning.

"Thank you," Meredith said quickly. "Thank you so much. I'm really very grateful, but I have to go." She flashed a quick smile over her shoulder as she hurried toward Mrs. Stinson.

"You're welcome!" he called after her.

Meredith quickened her pace.

"Hand your things to the driver and climb in quickly."

Mrs. Stinson slid onto the back seat of the car as the driver held out his arms for Meredith's suitcase.

"Thank you, sir," Meredith said as she dumped the bag into his arms. Her stocking dangled over the side. Meredith snatched it and stuffed it into her coat pocket.

The driver nodded at the open door of the car. He didn't look as stern as Mrs. Stinson—Meredith thought he might even have winked at her—but she didn't want to risk another scolding. She quickly slid onto the backseat beside Mrs. Stinson and pulled the door shut. The lid of the trunk slammed down. The driver settled into the front seat, and the car rumbled to life.

"You must not chatter to every boy you meet," Mrs. Stinson scolded. "I hope your aunt hasn't misled me."

Meredith bit back a reply. Mama always said, "Angry words are fuel to a fire," and Mrs. Stinson was near to blazing already.

As they bumped over the streetcar tracks, Meredith caught sight of the shoeshine boy waving to her from beside the newsstand. Meredith's heart lifted a little. People here in Toronto might not all be as unfriendly as Mrs. Stinson.

Meredith sat back and breathed in the rich, leathery smell of the upholstery. It reminded her of the saddles in Uncle Dan's barn back in Port Stuart. She sniffed happily until she realized sniffing was probably undignified. She didn't want to give Mrs. Stinson any more reason to think she was unsuitable. She stole a glance at Mrs. Stinson, who was looking out the window, one gloved finger tapping the side of her purse.

Meredith gazed out the window, too, hoping she looked like a serious and responsible fifteen-year-old girl with a job in Toronto. She wasn't fifteen, of course, but Mrs. Stinson didn't know that.

+++

"It's a good thing you're tall," Aunt Jane had said when she'd brought news that her husband's cousin had arranged a position in Toronto for Meredith. "Alma Stinson likes her girls to be fifteen."

Aunt Jane said Meredith was to remember that she was fifteen now, not thirteen, and that meant getting on with things and not dreaming the day away with her nose in some book.

"She's only a child, Jane," her mother said as she poured tea from the fat, brown teapot into the three china cups on the table. She pushed the one with the lilacs—Meredith's favorite—toward Aunt Jane.

"Mary Hollings, stop that nonsense! Stephen left you in an awful pickle. Meredith is old enough to take a job, and the war means there are plenty of jobs for girls who are eager for work." Aunt Jane frowned as she stirred her tea, the spoon racketing against the cup. "Ellen is six. She can get herself ready for school in the morning and help out more at home. You don't have any choice in the matter. Not if you want to pay off the debt Stephen racked up."

"I just hate that Meredith has to grow up so fast," Mama said, squeezing Meredith's hand. "And she has dreams of her own." Mama knew how much Meredith wanted to be a teacher.

"Nonsense!" Aunt Jane said that a lot. "It's high time she grew up. Alma places her girls with the very best families. There are plenty of others who would leap at the chance for a good job in Toronto. Those so-called dreams will have to wait."

"I suppose you're right." Mama squeezed Meredith's hand again and sighed.

Why did her mother always give in to Aunt Jane? One day Meredith was going to tell bossy Aunt Jane that she was an interfering busybody with too many opinions.

✚✚✚

Meredith stole another glance at the stern figure on the seat beside her. Mrs. Stinson's dark hair was arranged carefully under a little hat that exactly matched her navy coat, but she looked as sour as if something was pinching her.

I hope it *is*, thought Meredith. It made her feel better, but she knew that was mean and childish. Even though the last thing she wanted was to leave school and take a job so far from home, she needed to remember to be grown-up and respectful now.

But how had things gone wrong with Mrs. Stinson so quickly? Papa wouldn't have been surprised—his pet name for Meredith had been "Muddle." She missed him so much. She'd never get used to him being gone.

Meredith shook that thought out of her head and turned to Mrs. Stinson. Maybe conversation would help. "Is it far? To where we're going, I mean. This is my first time in Toronto."

"Anyone can see that," Mrs. Stinson said, although she wasn't looking at Meredith when she said it. She seemed intent on examining the tall houses lining the street. "It's about a twenty-minute drive to Rosedale."

"That's a wonderful name." Meredith imagined gardens filled with sunshine and overflowing with roses—pink climbing ones, wild ones that smelled like sugared apples and the red ones with thorns like daggers that the minister's wife grew back home. "Is it called Rosedale because so many roses grow there?"

"Rosedale is where the best families live," Mrs. Stinson said, as if that was all anyone needed to know and Meredith should have known it already.

"It sounds lovely," Meredith replied, but Mrs. Stinson's face was shut up tight like her purse. She was clearly not interested in conversation. Meredith hoped the people in Rosedale weren't all like Mrs. Stinson.

Meredith watched the city slide past the car window. Leaves tinged with red, orange and yellow lit the branches of the trees lining the street. Large houses—mansions, surely—of brick and stone, some with columns flanking their entrances, looked important and self-satisfied. They didn't look friendly like the houses in Port Stuart.

And so many people! Everyone looked dressed for church even though today was Monday. The men wore dark wool coats and smart bowler hats, the ladies were in elegant costumes with hats like swirls of icing atop fancy cakes. Meredith supposed there must be people in Toronto who had to make do with hand-me-downs, but she guessed they didn't live in Rosedale.

The knot that had been growing in her stomach ever since she left Port Stuart tightened. She rested her forehead against the cool glass of the car window.

+++

"You can't keep struggling, Mary. Stephen's been gone four years. And good riddance." Bossy Aunt Jane believed in plain speaking, but Meredith had hated her for that remark.

A salesman with the A. T. Clarkson Leather Company in Toronto, Stephen Hollings had breezed into

Port Stuart's general store on a sunny April afternoon.

"I go anywhere the train will take me," he'd boasted to the owner's two daughters behind the counter. Skeptical Jane thought he was a fast-talking no-account, but younger sister Mary was enchanted.

"And I thought," he told Meredith, with a wink, "that your mother was the prettiest brown-eyed girl in Ontario." They had married in June when Mary turned eighteen.

Meredith loved that story.

She'd been seven when Ellen was born and Granddad made his son-in-law an offer. "No more traipsing from town to town, Stephen. Your place is here with your family, and I need someone to run the business."

Aunt Jane had married Uncle Dan by then and moved to his family's farm. It was no secret that the store would go to Mary if her husband agreed to carry it on.

Meredith's father seemed to like his new responsibilities. "Nothing but pretty women coming in to see me every day," he'd say when he set off for the store each morning, "and even prettier ones waiting for me when I get home." But Meredith knew he missed his life on the road. Dull Port Stuart chafed him like a woolen shirt.

Things changed when Granddad died.

"It's 1914, Mary. This is all the rage in Toronto," Meredith's father would argue when Mama explained that local families couldn't afford the expensive items he ordered for the store. There was always too much of the wrong thing at the wrong time and not enough of the plain, everyday things folks wanted.

Meredith dreaded the quarreling that filled the house every night. She'd clamp her pillow over her head in the big double-bed she shared with Ellen, then strain to hear every word.

"I'm just wasting my time in this backwater!" Her father would be red-faced, his breath smelling of whiskey.

She tried her best to be helpful when Mama looked teary-eyed in the morning. She'd braid Ellen's long, brown hair and make their bed, and then clear the table without being asked. But Mama's smile wavered; she was not the laughing Mama Meredith remembered from before Granddad died.

One night, her father burst into the kitchen and flung the keys to the store onto the table. "It's yours by right, so take it. I'm sick of this place and everything in it."

There was a lot of arguing that night, and tears. And then, silence.

When her father tiptoed into her bedroom later that night, Meredith had squeezed her eyes shut so he'd think she was sleeping as soundly as Ellen. He smoothed her hair away from her forehead, then kissed them both and whispered, "Sleep tight, my girls."

She almost hugged him then, but a small voice inside

said that if she kept very still, maybe everything would be all right.

The creak of the hinge on the front door pulled her out of bed. From her bedroom window, Meredith watched her father stride away down the street. She stayed there long after the shadows swallowed the figure with the jaunty hat. She rested her wet cheek against the window frame and scratched at a bubble in the paint on the sill.

The telegram arrived four months later. Private First Class Stephen Hollings had been dead and buried before they knew he'd gone to war.

CHAPTER 3

The automobile turned in at a driveway flanked by stone gateposts. An ornate plaque proclaimed "Glenwaring" in flowing script. Meredith sat up straight and adjusted her hat, eager to see where she'd be working. Glenwaring, Rosedale and Toronto were so much more romantic than plain old Port Stuart.

Such a grand house! Six tall, white columns crowned with carved leaves. A veranda that stretched across the width of the house. An imposing wooden door. One, two, three stories, but the windows on the top floor were smaller. Meredith hoped her room would be up there—it would be like sleeping in the treetops.

The car drew to a stop in the circular driveway. Cheerful golden marigolds lined the sides of the path that led to the wide stone steps fronting the veranda.

"Quickly now." Mrs. Stinson stepped out of the car and headed up the path.

Meredith slid across the seat to follow her. The driver held out her suitcase—closed now, and looking perfectly respectable—and indicated she should follow Mrs. Stinson. Meredith took a deep breath and tightened her grip on the handle of her suitcase. She couldn't afford another accident. She started toward the house, her stomach fluttering.

"Harry Waterton!" The shout came from one side of the house. "Give it back!"

A small, blond boy raced around the corner of the house, straight at Meredith, a taller boy in pursuit.

"Oh!" Meredith cried as she leapt to the side, but the small boy swerved, too, and knocked her into the flowerbed.

He stared at Meredith in stunned silence.

Mama's hat sat upside down on the path. Meredith's hair had escaped its pins and a black curl dangled in front of her left eye. Her suitcase had landed in the flowerbed on the other side of the path. The medicinal smell of the crushed flowers made her stomach lurch. Meredith was sure Mrs. Stinson would march her straight back to Union Station and onto the first train home.

"Whoa, Harry! Damsel in distress!" The tall boy, grinning, offered her a not-quite-clean hand. Did every boy in Toronto think she was amusing?

"Thank you," she said through gritted teeth. "I'm fine." She ignored his outstretched hand, and got to her feet with as much dignity she could, brushing the dirt off her coat and skirt.

"Sorry about that," the tall boy said cheerfully. He was blond like the smaller one, and taller than she was. Meredith thought he must be fifteen at least. "Harry wasn't watching where he was going."

"It wasn't my fault!" Harry scowled. "I didn't see her."

"You need to get those eyes checked, Harry. You'll never be a flier with those bad eyes."

"I don't have bad eyes! I will too be a flier!" Harry ran headfirst at the tall boy, who plucked the airplane out of his grasp and held it overhead while Harry pummeled him.

"Margaret!" Mrs. Stinson called from the top of the steps, "What in heaven's name is keeping you?" Even the feathers on her navy hat seemed to be quivering with disapproval.

"Coming!" Meredith hastily scooped her own shabby hat from the path and righted her suitcase, thankful it hadn't popped open again. She hastened up the steps without another glance at the boys.

"This way." A thin, bald man dressed formally in a black jacket and white shirt held the big front door open. Meredith could see Mrs. Stinson waiting inside.

"Thank you," Meredith said to the man as she passed, but his stony expression didn't change. Another old crab—she crossed her fingers and hoped that she wouldn't be working for him.

In the front hall, a fire blazed in a hearth so large that her little sister could have easily stood inside. A large portrait above the mantel showed a blonde woman dressed in an elegant, pale-blue gown.

"Follow me, please," the man said to Mrs. Stinson.

"Straighten your hat, for heaven's sake," Mrs. Stinson whispered to Meredith before falling into step behind him.

Meredith settled her hat and followed, wishing she had a minute to compose herself. She didn't want them to think she was some small-town hobbledehoy who didn't know how to behave.

An angel holding a lantern crowned the intricately carved newel post at the bottom of a broad, curved staircase that swept to the second floor. Halfway up the stairs, a cozy window seat just perfect for reading on a rainy day sat under a stained-glass window. The many-branched chandelier suspended from the carved wooden ceiling high above cast dancing shadows on the wood-paneled walls.

The man led them through an archway and along a

paneled passage lined with electric lights. Meredith was careful not to knock her suitcase against the walls. As beautiful as it all was, she hoped she wouldn't be spending her days polishing acres of wood.

A growing aroma of cinnamon and fresh bread made Meredith's stomach growl. The sandwich she'd eaten on the train had been hours ago, and the peppermint stick didn't count.

"Here's the new girl, Mrs. Butters." The bald man held open the door at the end of the passage, and then stood to one side to let Mrs. Stinson and Meredith enter the kitchen.

A small, stout woman was taking something out of one of the ovens in the big black range set against one wall of the large room. She straightened as they entered, a pan in each hand.

"That's the last of them," she said, her face rosy from the heat as she tipped the loaves of bread out of their pans to join others cooling on racks on the long kitchen table. Her smooth, gray hair was caught in a bun at the back of her neck, and the large white apron that covered her front was dusted with flour. Meredith thought she looked like the gingerbread lady cookie cutter in the kitchen drawer back home.

"Hello, my dear. I'm Mrs. Butters," the woman said, taking Meredith's hand, her black eyes crinkling into a smile. "And you must be Margaret. We'll have to remember not to confuse you with our own Miss Maggie."

Meredith groaned inwardly. Not here, too. "Margaret" felt wrong and wrinkly, like wearing someone else's dress that didn't fit. She didn't want to start out by correcting Mrs. Butters, but she didn't want to be called Margaret either.

"And you've met Parker," Mrs. Butters said, nodding at the bald man.

"We have not, in fact, been properly introduced," Parker said, his face impassive. He extended his hand. "How do you do?"

Meredith set her suitcase down and shook his hand. His fingers were a clutch of bony twigs with no sign of warmth in them.

"How do you do?" she said, hoping for some answering friendliness, but Parker looked at her as if he didn't much like what he saw. She was surprised to see Mrs. Stinson nod at her with what might have been a smile. It seemed she'd finally done something right, but it didn't ease the knot in her stomach.

A scuffle, a bang, and then a howling Harry barreled into the kitchen. "Mrs. Butters! Jack won't let me play with his airplane!"

"Mr. Harry! Where are your manners?" Mrs. Butters crossed her arms over her chest.

Harry stopped in front of Meredith. "Are you the new one?"

"Manners, Mr. Harry, manners," Mrs. Butters said. "This is Margaret."

Meredith winced.

"She's come to work here now that Alice has gone," Mrs. Butters explained.

"I didn't like Alice," Harry said, glaring at Meredith. "She pinched me."

"You probably pinched her first, you devil." The tall boy—Jack—stood in the doorway, holding the model airplane.

"Did not!" cried Harry.

"Well, you probably kicked her, then," Jack said. "You've kicked all the others."

Harry ran at him, grabbing for the airplane, but Jack snatched it away.

"Mr. Jack! Mr. Harry! If you please!" Parker said, sharp as a strap across a palm.

The boys stopped.

"Mr. Jack, I suggest you give Mr. Harry the plane and take him outside," Parker said in a tone that implied he didn't expect an argument. He was clearly someone used to being obeyed. Meredith was glad he wasn't reprimanding her.

"But he'll break it!" Jack exclaimed. "I spent hours building it."

"Mr. Jack." Parker sighed. "Let me remind you that your father asked you to keep Mr. Harry busy until suppertime today. Mrs. Butters and I have some business to conclude."

"It's not fair! Why can't Maggie do it?" Jack scowled. "Besides, isn't this—," he motioned toward Meredith, "—Margaret girl here supposed to mind Harry?"

Except she wasn't Margaret. Even worse, Aunt Jane must have got the job wrong. Meredith stole a glance at Mrs. Stinson. Aunt Jane had told Mama that Meredith would be helping in the kitchen. She hadn't said anything about minding anyone, and certainly not anyone as unpleasant as Harry Waterton.

"All in good time, Mr. Jack," Mrs. Butters said, her hands on her hips, "but there won't be a suppertime tonight if you don't clear out and take Mr. Harry with you. You can take a cookie for each of you."

"Oh, all right." With one hand, Jack reached into a glass jar on the counter that held cookies. He grabbed his brother's arm with the other.

"Ow!" Harry cried. "I want a cookie!"

"Outside, pest," Jack said, towing a squirming Harry out of the room.

In the suddenly quiet kitchen, Parker turned to Mrs.

Stinson. "I'm terribly sorry, madam. Dr. Waterton could not be here this afternoon, and I'm afraid we've all been pushed right to the edge since Alice left."

"I understand completely," Mrs. Stinson said in a soothing voice, although her straight back and pursed-up mouth didn't look very understanding to Meredith. "There is simply no substitute for a loving mother, but Margaret will do her very best with young Harry."

Three pairs of eyes fastened on Meredith. She didn't know how she would keep that furious little hurricane in line. Harry was nothing like her sister Ellen—books and dolls wouldn't hold his attention for even a minute. Back home, she'd told herself that working in Toronto would be an adventure. Now it looked like it might be a mistake.

Parker cleared his throat. "Listen carefully, Margaret."

If she was going to work here, Meredith thought, she just couldn't be called Margaret. She wiped her suddenly sweaty hands on her coat.

"You will primarily work with Mrs. Butters in the kitchen, but you will have other duties in the household," Parker was saying. "Mrs. Butters will explain those to you. And you are to help with Mr. Harry as needed, under Mrs. Butters' direction. You will report to her on those matters."

He looked at her, eyebrows raised, and Meredith nodded, even though she hadn't really taken in much of what he said. Her stomach felt squeezed into a too-small space.

"There will, of course, be times when I require your assistance," Parker continued, "and then you will report directly to me. Do I make myself clear, Margaret?"

She had to set them straight right now. If she left it any longer it would be too late. Meredith opened her mouth, but no sound came out.

Parker leaned toward her. "I repeat: do I make myself clear?"

"Don't stand there gawping, Margaret," Mrs. Stinson said.

Meredith swallowed hard. "It's Meredith!" she squeaked.

Parker's eyes narrowed. Mrs. Butters' eyebrows knit together.

"I'm not Margaret, I'm Meredith," Meredith said in a rush. "Meredith Hollings."

Parker looked at Mrs. Butters, and then they both looked at Mrs. Stinson, who looked as if she'd swallowed something nasty.

"Did I say 'Margaret'?" Mrs. Stinson tittered. "How silly of me. I meant 'Meredith,' of course."

Now Mrs. Stinson's face was red. Meredith would have liked to savor that, but she was watching Parker and Mrs. Butters, hoping that they understood, worrying that they might think she'd been rude.

"Meredith Hollings," Parker said carefully, as if he couldn't quite fit his mouth around such an outlandish name.

"Welcome to Glenwaring, Meredith," Mrs. Butters said, smiling. "We're glad you're here."

"Sundays free and Wednesday afternoons as arranged." Mrs. Stinson was all business now. "One weekend free each month. Wages paid on Fridays." She turned to Meredith. "And, of course, impeccable behavior at all times."

"No suitors." Parker said firmly. "Is that understood?"

"Yes, sir," Meredith replied. Imagine him thinking she'd have suitors! He must think she really was fifteen after all.

"Yes, *Parker*," he said.

He was cross with her already! "Yes, Parker," she repeated.

"Not a scrap of training." Parker shook his head. "Mrs. Stinson, Dr. Waterton clearly stated—"

"Don't worry, Meredith." Mrs. Butters said warmly. "You'll soon have the way of it."

Meredith let out a breath she didn't know she'd been holding. She suited kind Mrs. Butters, if no one else. The knot in her stomach loosened for the first time since she'd stepped off the train.

"Then we're settled," Parker said. "As long as you're satisfied, Mrs. Butters?"

"Absolutely," Mrs. Butters said. "Meredith looks like a capable young lady."

Meredith could have hugged her.

Mrs. Stinson consulted the small gold watch pinned to her lapel. "Look at the time! I really must be going. Tell Dr. Waterton I'll call next week." She pulled on her gloves and turned to Meredith. "Impeccable behavior," she cautioned, as though Meredith might start a ruckus at any minute.

Meredith watched Parker escort Mrs. Stinson out of the kitchen. She was glad to see the back of that unpleasant woman but was worried that Parker would turn out to be worse.

Surely the kitchen of a house as big as this would have lots to keep her busy! And even though she wasn't looking forward to it, minding Harry Waterton meant she likely wouldn't spend much time with crosspatch Parker.

Toronto might just turn out to be an adventure after all.

CHAPTER 4

"Hang your coat and hat on a hook by the back door, Meredith," Mrs. Butters said once they were alone, "and we'll have a cup of tea." She filled the kettle and set it to boil on the big, black range with its bewildering array of doors.

Tall windows poured late-afternoon light into the kitchen. The clay-colored walls and gray-green cupboards were like a much-washed quilt wrapped around the room. A scuttle heaped with coal squatted beside the range. Pots and pans had been stacked on the counter beside a wide, grey stone sink set under the windows—waiting for her, Meredith guessed.

"Meredith's an unusual name for a girl." Mrs. Butters took a plate from the large painted dresser against one wall, and filled it with cookies from the jar on the counter. "It's Welsh, I think. Is your family Welsh?" She set out two china cups and saucers with cheerful yellow roses around the rim.

"My Granddad was from Wales. I'm named for him," Meredith said, her eyes on the plate of cookies. She hoped Mrs. Butters couldn't hear her growling stomach.

"That explains it, then," Mrs. Butters said. She spooned tea from a tin canister into a sturdy, brown teapot, and then poured in boiling water from the kettle. "And where are you from, Meredith?"

"Port Stuart," Meredith said, "on Lake Erie. My Granddad had a general store. My mother runs it now."

"Sit down, my dear. We'll let that steep a minute." Mrs. Butters settled into a chair at one end of the table. "A general store, you say?"

Meredith took the chair nearest Mrs. Butters. "Yes, ma'am." Those cookies looked tasty.

"Port Stuart's quite a distance. I'll bet you're hungry." Mrs. Butters pushed the plate of cookies closer to Meredith.

Meredith reached eagerly for a cookie. Its sugar-and-cinnamon smell whisked her back to the wooden spice bins in Mama's store where she would scoop spices into tiny brown bags. Their exotic aromas were like messages from places that never had winter.

She hadn't meant to eat the first cookie so quickly. "May I please have another?"

"Of course," Mrs. Butters said. "You've nice manners, Meredith. Still, you're a skinny thing, even if you're nearly as tall as Mr. Jack. How old are you, dear?"

Meredith arranged her face into an expression she hoped looked serious and responsible. "I'm—I'm fifteen." She tried to take smaller bites, but the second cookie was as delicious as the first. She reached for another.

"Good gracious, you certainly are hungry! And probably still growing," Mrs. Butters said. "However, I suppose some people look young for their age. Why don't I set out a bit of cheese, too, and slice up some of this bread?"

Mrs. Butters set about slicing bread and shaving cheese from a block on the dresser. "As Parker said, you'll mainly work here in the kitchen with me," she explained, "but you'll help keep an eye on young Mr. Harry when he's not in school."

Meredith hoped her face wasn't revealing how she felt about that. "Where's Mrs. Waterton?"

"Mrs. Waterton, bless her, died a year ago April. Everyone's taken it very hard. Mr. Harry had just turned five, poor lamb. He's in school now and that helps keep him busy. He can certainly be a handful, but I guess you know that by now."

"What about Ja—Mr. Jack?"

"Mr. Jack was devastated. He still gets angry at the smallest thing, and he's older than Miss Maggie. She's thirteen, and a girl needs her mother. She's always been difficult but now..." Mrs. Butters sighed. "Never mind. You'll see for yourself soon enough."

Meredith could not imagine losing her mama. It had been hard when Papa had left. At first, Meredith had clung to the hope he'd come back one day. The telegram, when it had come, had been terrible enough, and she'd known she'd always miss him, but through it all she and Ellen had still had Mama.

"You'll help Parker wait table and serve when there are guests for dinner," Mrs. Butters said as she set the plate of bread and cheese in front of Meredith.

Waiting table would be more fun than scrubbing pots or running after cross little boys. Meredith hoped there'd be lots of dinner guests. She sandwiched three slices of cheese between two pieces of bread, her mouth watering.

"Parker's the butler," Mrs. Butters continued, pouring more tea into Meredith's cup, "and Forrest—the man who drove you here—is chauffeur and gardener and handyman all rolled into one. Mrs. O'Hagan comes every weekday to clean and does the laundry on Mondays."

Meredith wondered why they said "Mrs. Butters" and "Mrs. O'Hagan," but not "Mr. Parker" or "Mr. Forrest."

What others things like that might trip her up and land her in trouble with Parker?

"Now, my dear, have you had any experience?"

Meredith's stomach fluttered. "This is my first real job," she said slowly, "but I did a lot of the cooking and housework at home and looked after my sister when Mama was at the store."

"Then I'm sure you'll do just fine," Mrs. Butters said. She poured more tea into her own cup. The kitchen was darkening as afternoon slid into evening. "Your Mama runs the store? I suppose your father's in the army.

"My son, Ben, is in France," she continued before Meredith could answer. "Terrible sick they've been, with this Spanish Flu, but he's been lucky so far. Is your father overseas?" Her bright, black eyes were full of questions.

"Papa was in the army," Meredith said, "but—" She blinked hard and focused her eyes on a long scratch across the top of the wooden table.

"Oh, my dear," Mrs. Butters said after a moment. She reached for Meredith's hand and took it in her own warm one. "I'm sorry. I didn't think. It's a dreadful time for so many families."

Meredith nodded. The lump in her throat made it hard to swallow.

"That's more than enough chatting for one afternoon," Mrs. Butters said briskly, getting to her feet. "Dr.

Waterton likes his dinner promptly at seven." She carried the cookie plate and her cup-and-saucer over to the sink. "Take that apron by the door, and you can start on the potatoes. My Aunt Hester used to say that busy hands heal troubled hearts, and it's the best medicine I know."

Meredith hastily wiped her eyes as she crossed the kitchen. She took a large, white apron off the hook and tied it over her dress—her best dress, but that couldn't be helped. Mrs. Butters handed her a paring knife and pointed to the basket of potatoes she'd placed beside the sink.

I'd rather sell potatoes than peel them, Meredith thought as she dug the eyes out of a particularly knobby specimen, but peeling potatoes meant she'd be sending money home. She'd think of the potatoes as pennies, magic pennies piling up to pay what they owed. Maybe then, if she wasn't too old and hadn't forgotten everything, she'd find a way to finish school and be a teacher. Papa always said anything was possible if you believed hard enough. And no school board would want to hire a potato-peeling pot scrubber who'd left school before she turned fourteen.

Meredith dropped the peeled potato into the pot Mrs. Butters had set beside her and picked up another. Long tails of peel unwound from her hands and mounded into a soggy, brown mass on the counter in front of her as she filled the pot with potatoes that didn't look one bit like magic pennies.

She'd have to do a powerful lot of believing.

CHAPTER 5

Sunlight slid over the windowsill early the next morning and illuminated the tiny, pink rosebuds on the wallpaper in Meredith's room. At first, she couldn't remember where she was or why Ellen wasn't in bed beside her, but then she remembered the long train ride the day before.

The washstand that sat at the foot of the bed held a china jug and basin, and a small, white towel hung from the rail across the top. Meredith's suitcase sat beside the washstand. On the other side of the window, an oval mirror just big enough for her to see her face was tacked to the wall, above a small dresser with three drawers and glass knobs that looked like chunks of ice. Her stockings and underclothes huddled on a wooden chair on the far side of the dresser. Her coat and hat and the dress she'd worn the day before hung from hooks beside the door.

Meredith sat up and hugged her arms close. The fall morning was cold despite her flannel nightgown. She hopped out of bed, snatched her things from the chair and scooted back under the faded, pink coverlet on the bed. She shrugged out of her nightgown and wriggled into her underclothes and stockings in the warm cave underneath the covers, the way she and Ellen did at home.

Maybe Ellen was getting dressed now, too. Mama would be making breakfast. Soon, Ellen would come racketing down the stairs and Mama would have to remind her to set the table like she did every morning—

Better not think about home too much. Meredith slid down to the end of the bed, the coverlet tucked around her, and reached for her suitcase. She'd been so tired last night she hadn't unpacked. One of her everyday dresses would be better for kitchen work. She pulled out her favorite with its green-and-brown stripes, glad it still fit even though she'd grown so much this year. She didn't mind that the twelve, tiny buttons down the front took forever to fasten, but finally they were closed and she pulled on the soft, green sweater Mama had knit for her last winter. Meredith had loved hearing the *clickety-clack* of Mama's knitting needles every evening after the dishes were done. The sweater would keep Mama close to her all day.

Meredith felt under the bed for her clunky brown

school shoes. She shouldn't call them "school shoes" now that she'd left school, but calling them something else wouldn't take away their ugliness.

"Never mind," Mama had said while Meredith polished them the night before her trip to Toronto. "You're to take your very first wages to Mr. Eaton's store and buy yourself a brand-new pair."

Mrs. Stinson had said Meredith's wages would be paid on Fridays. Would she have earned enough for shoes in four days' time? Just as soon as she could, she'd go to Mr. Eaton's store and look at shoes anyway. That way she could take her time deciding on what she wanted, like any grand lady in Rosedale.

She quickly made the bed, arranged her few things in the dresser, and placed her Bible on top, wishing she had a book to set beside the Bible so she could lose herself in a story at bedtime. She'd ask Mrs. Butters if there was a lending library nearby.

Meredith shook her hair out of its nighttime braid and tugged her wooden-handled hairbrush through her thick curls. She bundled it into a knot at the back of her head with the hairpins that reminded her of the long-legged herons that stalked the marshy shores near Port Stuart.

Meredith studied the serious face looking back at her from the mirror: eyebrows like smears of black paint above brown eyes flecked with gold, a nose peppered with freckles, black hair that snaked its way out of imprisonment no matter how securely she pinned it. A wide open face, Papa had called it.

"I miss Papa," she whispered to the girl in the mirror, "and now I miss Mama and Ellen, too." But the girl in the mirror couldn't offer any comfort and there was no point wishing things were different.

Meredith moved to the window. Her room was on the third floor and it really was like sleeping in the treetops! Tree-lined streets wound in all directions, thin columns of smoke marking where houses sat under the canopy of colorful leaves. Church spires poked into the sky: big ones nearby, small ones in the distance. Pigeons pecked companionably at the ground below her window, their throaty noises like the voices of the women back home tidying up after a church supper.

That sparkle in the distance had to be Lake Ontario. From Port Stuart, you could sail all the way along the shores of Lake Erie and Lake Ontario to Toronto. She really wasn't so far away if she could follow the shoreline home.

A knock sounded on the door. "Meredith? Are you awake?"

Meredith hurried to open it. Mrs. Butters stood panting in the hallway; her rosy cheeks making her look even more like a gingerbread lady. "Good gracious, all those stairs! I don't come up here as often as I should. I forgot to give you an alarm clock—Alice took the old one with her, if you can believe it."

"Am I late?" Surely not on her very first morning.

"Don't fret. I'm sure you needed the sleep, but tomorrow you'll need to be up early to stoke the stove so it's hot when I arrive at seven." Mrs. Butters led the way down the narrow staircase, puffing a little, her carpet slippers scuffing on the wooden stairs. "You'll need to go quietly in the mornings so you don't wake the family," she said as they reached the second-floor landing, "although today everyone's up ahead of you."

Meredith vowed silently she'd be on time tomorrow as they descended the last flight of stairs to the kitchen, where an argument was raging over the remains of breakfast.

"Listen to this," Forrest quoted from the newspaper on the table in front of him, "*There is altogether too much made of the seriousness of this Spanish Influenza.*" His face was florid under white hair that stood up in spikes as if he'd just run his hand through it. "Can you believe the cheek?"

Meredith remembered the newspaper man calling out something about the Spanish Flu the day before, and Mrs. Butters had mentioned it, too. In Port Stuart, letters from the men overseas had told of it, but no one she knew overseas had fallen ill so far. She slipped into an empty chair at the other end of the table.

Parker's eyes traveled from Meredith to the big kitchen clock and back again. He wasn't about to tell her not to fret. Maybe if she got up extra early all week, he'd forget about her being late today.

"The epidemic is not so serious as measles," Forrest continued, *"and while a few deaths have occurred among the Poles at Camp Niagara, everything possible has been done to prevent the spread."*

"That's exactly right." Parker calmly buttered a piece of toast. "This so-called Spanish Influenza has been confined to the army overseas and the odd case at the training camps over here. It hasn't yet been reliably reported in Toronto. We're in no danger." His bald head bobbed as he spoke, like the pigeons Meredith had seen from her window upstairs.

"But some have died from it, man!" Forrest persisted. "What's more dangerous than that?"

"Hush now, you two," Mrs. Butters said, spooning something into a bowl from a pot on the range. "You'll scare Meredith if you keep on like that."

Parker plucked the newspaper from Forrest's hands and studied it. "And if you'd kept on reading," he said, ignoring Mrs. Butters, "you'd have seen this: '*As far as I can learn, there is no pathological difference between plain influenza and the so-called Spanish variety,' said Dr. Hallowfield.*" He dabbed his napkin at the corners of his mouth. "I see no need to panic."

"Dr. Waterton says it's only a matter of time before it spreads into the city." Forrest reached for a piece of toast.

"Then I'm afraid he's wrong," Parker said, cutting his toast into neat squares.

"And just where did you do your medical training, Parker?" Forrest asked.

"Don't listen to them," Mrs. Butters said to Meredith as she set a steaming bowl of porridge in front of her. "They go on like that all day. It's enough to make your head spin. There's toast on the table and tea in the pot."

Meredith reached for the teapot and filled her mug.

"I trust you will not make a habit of sleeping in," Parker said, frowning at Meredith as if she'd woken up late just to vex him.

"I'm sorry," she said. Serious and responsible, she reminded herself. And polite. Especially to Parker. "I'll be on time from now on."

"Leave the girl alone," Forrest said, winking at Meredith. "She's only just arrived."

"I prefer to nip bad habits in the bud." Parker leaned toward Forrest. "Remember Alice," he said in a voice that painted Alice as something very bad indeed.

"Let's not remember Alice!" Mrs. Butters exclaimed,

pausing between the stove and the pantry. "Meredith is here now, and she's a nice, polite girl and a hard worker." Her black eyes flashed a challenge that made Parker look away.

He doesn't want to get on Mrs. Butters' bad side the way Alice clearly had, thought Meredith. All the same, she wasn't going to waste her sympathy on him. She looked for the sugar bowl only to see it disappear over the edge of the table, seemingly under its own power. She slid her chair back and peered underneath the table.

Harry Waterton was sitting cross-legged on the floor, rapidly spooning sugar into his mouth, his eyes closed in utter bliss.

"Stop that!" Meredith whispered fiercely.

Harry's eyes flew open and the spoon clattered to the floor.

Mrs. Butters' head appeared below the table top. "Mr. Harry! Come out of there at once!"

The little boy crawled out slowly. Sugar coated the front of his navy-blue sweater.

"You've no business hiding in my kitchen, young man. How long have you been down there?" Mrs. Butters shook her finger at the little boy.

Meredith bit back a giggle. Forrest laughed, and even Parker managed a pained smile.

"And sugar is scarce, as you well know," Mrs. Butters

scolded, barely pausing for breath. "If you take more than your share, our brave soldiers don't have what they need to win the war. You should be ashamed of yourself. Don't let me find you hiding in here again!" She marched the small boy to the door. "Now scoot back to the dining room. Did no one notice you were gone?"

Meredith caught Forrest's eye. He grinned.

"Good gracious, he's a handful," Mrs. Butters said, shaking her head. "Always at the sugar. Boys will be boys, I suppose."

"Girls, too," Meredith said. "My little sister is always trying to sneak some sugar."

"All the same, I'd choose Harry's escapades over Maggie's tantrums any day," Forrest said. He got to his feet, brushing crumbs from his trousers.

"I will agree with you on that point, Forrest," Parker said with an odd little cackle that made Meredith wonder if he was making a joke. "Harry may be a handful, but Maggie's a menace."

"Finish up, Meredith," Mrs. Butters said as the men put their jackets on, "and then you can clear the dining room."

Meredith quickly spooned up her porridge, making sure there was sugar in every spoonful. Even though she liked the way it smelled, porridge was just plain nasty without sugar.

It seemed to her that Glenwaring was like the harbor in Port Stuart with vessels of all kinds passing through. Mrs. Butters was a cheerful tugboat chugging this way and that, looking after all the other boats. Forrest was a ferry, of course, taking people here and there. Harry was a cheeky little rowboat, and Jack could only be a plane—an airship—soaring over Lake Ontario.

Her imagination stopped short at Parker. It almost spoiled the game to include him. But then it came to her: a battleship—all cold, gray iron, and laden with rules and procedures.

And I'm a raft that's floated safely all the way to Toronto, Meredith thought. I'm not going to let myself get swamped by that baleful old battleship.

CHAPTER 6

A few minutes later, tray in hand, Meredith waited in the hallway outside the dining room. Through the doorway, she could see Jack and an older man, who could only be Dr. Waterton, sitting at a table that could have easily seated twelve. Meredith thought it must take hours to polish the curlicues on the ornate chairs set around the table.

The rich red of the dining room walls glowed in the morning sunlight streaming through the large windows. There was no sign of Harry—or Maggie, Meredith realized, disappointed. She was eager to get a glimpse of the one thing Parker and Forrest agreed on.

"The official word," Dr. Waterton was saying to his son, pointing to the newspaper, "is that there's no cause for alarm. But I'm afraid it may be more serious than anyone realizes."

Meredith was close enough to see that the doctor's plate of eggs and bacon looked untouched. Should she knock? Enter without knocking? Mama would say she shouldn't be listening like this, but Mrs. Butters had sent her to clear the dishes. Did that mean she should start clearing right away or wait until they left the room? She hadn't thought to ask.

"I don't know why you're telling me this." Jack's back was to Meredith, so she couldn't see his face, but the tone of his voice was sulky.

"Because you're nearly sixteen, Jack. It's time you took an interest if you're going to be a doctor."

"I'm not going to be a doctor. I'm going to be a pilot."

"Not that flying nonsense again!" The doctor dropped the newspaper onto the table, knocking over his coffee cup.

Meredith darted forward. Her tray clattered to the floor as she grabbed the empty cup that was rolling toward the edge of the table. For a scary moment she thought she was going to end up in the doctor's lap.

"Good heavens!" Dr. Waterton drew back as Meredith righted herself.

Jack laughed. "She was upside down in the flowerbed yesterday!"

"I'm sorry, sir." Meredith set the cup back onto the saucer and stepped back. Her dratted hair had come loose and she could feel herself blushing. "Mrs. Butters sent me to clear the table. Should I come back later?"

"And spoil that entrance?" Dr. Waterton chuckled. His sandy hair was thinning on top, and his eyes looked kind behind their gold-rimmed spectacles. "You're a definite improvement over the last one. What's your name?"

"Meredith Hollings, sir."

Dr. Waterton got to his feet. To Meredith's relief, he didn't seem angry in the least. "Pleased to meet you, Meredith."

She was so delighted he'd got her name right that it took her a moment to realize he'd extended his hand. She hesitated, and then shook it shyly.

"Finding your way around all right?" Dr. Waterton removed his spectacles and tucked them into a pocket in his gray silk vest.

"Yes, sir. Everyone's been very kind." Almost everyone, she amended silently as she stooped to retrieve the fallen tray.

"Glad to hear it." Dr. Waterton turned to his son. "Don't be late for school, Jack. And think about what I said. You need to keep your grades up."

"I'm never late," Jack replied. "It's a waste of time to

arrive before the bell rings." He bunched his napkin into a ball as he got to his feet and tossed it past Meredith's head onto the sideboard. "See you later, Meredith-not-Margaret," he said from the doorway.

A pretty, blonde girl pushed past him and planted herself in front of the doctor. "Papa, Abby's mother is taking her shopping today and they've invited me. Please say I can go!"

Her long hair was held back by a band of green plaid that matched her pleated skirt and the tie on her trim, white blouse. She looked as dainty as a porcelain doll from the Eaton's catalogue.

"You mean you want to miss a day of school, Maggie." The doctor sighed.

"That's not fair!" Jack protested. "I have to keep my grades up and she gets a day off?"

"Jack!" Dr. Waterton exclaimed. "This doesn't involve you. Go find Harry and make sure he's got his books and coat."

Jack slouched away, grumbling. Meredith concentrated on making no noise as she added a side plate and serving platter to the tray she had set on the table. She didn't think she should be hearing this conversation either, but no one seemed to mind that she was in the room.

"I won't be missing anything, Papa," Maggie said,

smiling sweetly up at her father. "We're only doing review right now and—"

"And your last school report was dreadful," Dr. Waterton said. "Missing school is out of the question."

"But Abby's mother doesn't mind if Abby misses a day. Besides, I can get Abby a gift for her birthday party next week so we won't have to do that another day. Just this once? Can I? Please?"

"You're not Abby, my girl, and the answer is still no," the doctor said. "Get your things and you can ride along with Harry and me as far as your school, if you like. I'll have Forrest bring the car around."

The air in the dining room churned with an angry silence after he left. Meredith could feel Maggie's eyes on her as she added the sugar bowl and creamer to her tray. She wondered whether she was to take the salt cellar and pepper grinder to the kitchen with the dishes or whether they should go on the sideboard.

"Who wants to go to boring old school?" Maggie complained. "I bet you're glad to be finished with it."

"Oh, no," Meredith said, pausing in her journey between the table and the sideboard to turn toward Maggie. "I liked school."

"Boring figures, and boring grammar, and the boring, old kings and queens of boring, old England? You liked that?"

"Oh, yes," Meredith said, wistfully. "It was much better than taking care of my sister, or helping in the store, or washing pots—"

Had she said too much? Imagine telling Maggie Waterton that she didn't like kitchen work! She set a stack of plates on the tray. It was time to get on with her work. "If you'll excuse me, Miss Maggie—"

"Don't call me that!" Maggie's face was a thundercloud.

"I'm sorry. Did I say something wrong?"

"That name!" Maggie stood scowling, her hands on her hips. "I hate it!"

"You mean 'Miss Maggie'?" Meredith had definitely heard everyone else say it. She couldn't think how she'd gotten it wrong.

"Yes, I mean 'Miss Maggie'!" Her face was now scarlet as a zinnia. "You are to call me 'Miss Margaret.'"

"But they all—"

"I'm thirteen, much too old for a baby name like Maggie. How would you like being called by a name you hate?"

"Oh, I wouldn't like it at all," Meredith said, eagerly. "I know exactly how you feel. As a matter of fact—"

"I doubt," Maggie said, her ice-blue eyes taking in the tray, the apron, the homemade sweater, "you know exactly how I feel."

Mama always said it was the person that counted,

not where they came from or what they had, but it seemed that was different in Rosedale, too.

"I'm sorry," Meredith said quietly. "I'll get it right the next time."

The blue eyes narrowed. "See that you do."

"Maggie!" Dr. Waterton called from the hall. "Are you coming?"

"Papa!" Maggie stamped her foot. "I've told you not to call me that!" She flounced out of the dining room.

Meredith seethed as she carried the laden tray out of the dining room and along the passage to the kitchen. Maggie—no, *Miss Margaret*—had nice things to wear, her room was probably filled with books she didn't read, and she didn't have to leave school to work in someone else's house in a strange city. That stuck-up girl didn't know how lucky she was.

CHAPTER 7

Meredith sat on the back step the next evening, grateful for the cool night air bathing her face. Her hands were raw from scrubbing the dishes that piled up endlessly by the sink. Chopping and stirring and mixing were fun, but she hated washing dishes.

And keeping an eye on Harry wore her out. Luckily, he loved being in the kitchen with Mrs. Butters, who let him chop and stir and mix alongside Meredith. It seemed that keeping them busy was also Mrs. Butters' formula for keeping small boys out of trouble. Meredith tried not to begrudge Harry his messes, even though she was the one who had to clean them up.

But then, with no warning, Harry would vanish. She'd lost count of how many times Mrs. Butters had told her to stop what she was doing to go and find him. He delighted in finding new places to hide, even though Mrs. Butters scolded him for taking Meredith away from her work. Once in a while, he would sit still long enough for Meredith to tell him a story, but then his inexhaustible motor would roar to life again. She was thankful when Mrs. Butters finally coaxed him upstairs to bed.

But minding Harry wasn't her worst problem.

"You must not disappear," Parker had scolded when he'd heard her tell Mrs. Butters that she was going upstairs to get her sweater.

"You must not clomp like a farm girl," he'd complained when she'd tried to walk quickly—and that after he'd fussed about how long she took to get from the kitchen to the dining room.

"You must not dilly-dally," he'd lectured when all she'd been doing was glancing through the newspaper. In fact, Parker had seemed surprised that she could read at all, as if not reading was something else that had been passed on from Alice.

He was a dried-up, meddling, know-it-all fusspot! Meredith's fingers itched to pinch Parker's sharp nose when it pointed in her direction.

She plucked a scarlet-edged leaf from the shrub beside the step and rolled it between her fingers. Never mind, she told herself, you're out of his reach for a few minutes anyway. Don't let him spoil this time, too.

Faint automobile sounds drifted toward her. Across the yard, she could just make out a woman moving in the kitchen of the house beside Glenwaring, clearing up after supper, no doubt. Meredith had been glad to escape Parker and Forrest in one of their endless arguments at Glenwaring's kitchen table.

"It's folly," Forrest had insisted. "Pure folly. They should close them all: schools, theaters—churches, even."

The Spanish Flu, again. Desperate for something to read, Meredith had been ducking into the pantry to read the newspaper whenever she had a few free minutes. It was filled with lengthy, and scary, accounts of Spanish Influenza sweeping across American cities. Some reports said it had reached Montreal. No one seemed to agree on whether the people of Toronto might fall prey to it soon.

"Dr. Hallowfield has said repeatedly that there's absolutely no cause for anxiety," Parker had told her just that afternoon when he'd discovered her reading in the pantry. "He's the top man in the city's Department of Public Health. He says healthy people should walk more, not crowd into the streetcars, and avoid anything that might bring on a cold. You're in no danger here."

Then he'd said that if she had so much free time that she could be reading in the middle of the work day, she most certainly had time to polish all the shoes in the back hall.

Meredith's shoulder still ached from the vigorous polishing Parker had demanded. She couldn't imagine why one family needed so many shoes. Maggie Waterton could wear a different pair every day of the week, while Meredith had to make do with one battered pair so scuffed that no amount of polishing would ever make them shine. The prospect of buying new shoes at Mr. Eaton's store was Meredith's one bright spot in the endless round of dish-washing that filled her days.

All the same, Meredith knew Mama would be reading about the Spanish Flu in the Toronto papers and worrying. Meredith decided to write a letter home that night to reassure her. Meredith was working in a doctor's house, for goodness sake! What could be safer than that?

Forrest pounded the kitchen table. "What about Boston? They didn't think they had the Spanish Flu, and now there are hundreds—*thousands*—ill."

"One of the hospital trustees recently visited Boston and saw the Spanish Flu there firsthand," Parker replied, in that infuriatingly calm tone that said 'I know better than you.' "He said Toronto is experiencing only a slightly more serious strain of the usual grippe."

Meredith hoped he was right. If Toronto was safe from the Spanish Flu, then maybe Port Stuart would be, too. She couldn't bear to think of Mama or Ellen sick when she herself was stuck here, trying to keep on the good side of miserable Parker and to avoid hateful Maggie.

Just that afternoon, Maggie and her friend Abby had been giggling together about a party and boys. They'd fallen silent when they caught sight of Meredith, their eyes examining her as if she were some horrible species of insect. After she passed them, Meredith heard fierce whispering and laughter.

Remembering that, Meredith felt angry all over again. Mama would have been appalled at such bad manners. "Be kind," Mama often reminded her. "You never know what troubles someone might have."

Meredith didn't care about Maggie's troubles, and she cared even less about Parker's. Papa would have called the two of them "hoity-toities," his term for customers who treated shopkeepers like servants.

"Hello, Meredith-not-Margaret. Aren't you cold?"

Meredith started at the sudden voice from behind. She turned her head to see Jack Waterton slouched against the doorframe, smiling down at her.

"Not really," she said. He made her uncomfortable, hovering like that. She tried to stand, but her skirt was caught on something and she got stuck halfway. She tugged at her skirt, gently at first, then harder, but it wouldn't come free. Flustered, she bent down to see what was catching it and discovered Jack's foot firmly planted on the hem of her skirt.

"Please," Meredith said. "You're standing on my skirt." She tried to work it free.

"I'll step off if you promise not to go in," Jack said. Something in his tone made her look up. "Stay and talk to me," he said, his bright blue eyes holding hers.

Meredith darted a look to the kitchen where Parker and Forrest were still arguing.

"Please?" Jack said.

Meredith decided it would be nice to talk to someone who was older than six and wasn't ordering her to do something.

"All right," she said, "but only for a few minutes. I have to be up early."

She sat back down on the step and Jack lifted his foot. As he settled himself beside her, she tucked her dress firmly around her legs, wrapped her arms around her knees and shifted away from him. She could feel him looking at her, but she made her own eyes trace the striped pattern on her dress.

"Lots of stars tonight," Jack said at last. "Should be clear tomorrow. Good weather for flying."

"Are you going flying?" Meredith had seen airplanes in the sky above Port Stuart occasionally, but she'd never seen one up close.

"No. Wish I was, though. I will when I'm eighteen, if the war lasts that long."

"You're going to be a pilot?" She could picture Jack in a leather jacket and cap, a white scarf around his neck, goggles pushed to the top of his head like the pictures she'd seen in the newspaper. She had to admit he'd look dashing.

Jack shrugged. "I have to be eighteen before they'll take me."

"The boys at home all played at being pilots fighting the Germans." Meredith smiled, remembering.

"Did anyone want to be the Germans?" Jack leaned back on his elbows and looked at her.

"No, they drew straws for that."

Jack laughed. Light from the open doorway behind them spilled onto the path that led to the stable, making the step they were sitting on an island in a pool of light. Meredith hugged her knees and glanced toward the kitchen again. Parker would no doubt say it wasn't proper to be sitting out here with Jack Waterton, but now she was reluctant to go in. She wondered what Jack was thinking.

"Do you like it here?" he asked, leaning toward her. His straight blond hair fell across his forehead.

Goodness! Meredith tried to shift farther away from him along the step, but she was already right at the edge. "Liking isn't part of it," she said. "It's hard work, but Mrs.

Butters is kind and I'm learning a lot."

"Wouldn't you rather do something you liked?"

"Sometimes you do things because you have to. It doesn't matter whether you like them or not." She stole a glance at Jack's face. She wasn't sure that had come out right. She didn't want him to think she was silly.

"When I'm eighteen, I'm going to do what I like," Jack announced. "And it won't be studying to be a doctor, even though that's what my father wants." He studied her, a small wrinkle between his eyebrows. "You're old enough to be working, so why can't you choose? How old are you, anyway?"

"Fifteen." Meredith's cheeks burned. She wanted to put some distance between them, but if she moved any farther she'd fall into the bushes.

"Only fifteen? What about high school?"

"My family needs me to work." Meredith hoped that sounded grown-up. "My aunt knew Mrs. Stinson, and she knew about this job, so here I am."

If only he'd stop looking at her.

"I should go in," she said, standing up quickly—no snag this time—and smoothing her skirt.

Jack scrambled to his feet and blocked her path to the door. "Then we're the same age," he said, a smile touching the corners of his mouth, "for a few days more, anyway. When's your birthday?" His hand brushed hers.

"I have to go." Meredith tried to slip past him, but she stumbled over the shoes on the mat inside the door and nearly lost her balance.

"Steady!" Jack grabbed her arm. His hand burned through her sleeve. He was too close, crowding her, and suddenly there wasn't enough air even though the door was wide open.

Meredith pulled her arm from his grasp and stepped away. Her heart was pounding so hard she was sure he could hear it.

"My shoes," Jack said, after a long moment. He picked up the battered pair of black shoes that had been covered in mud before she polished them that afternoon. "I came for my rugger shoes." He headed for the kitchen, swinging the shoes by their laces, without a backward glance.

Meredith stood beside the open door, the night air washing over her, looking past Jack Waterton to where Parker sat at the kitchen table, watching them both.

CHAPTER 8

Meredith held the candle as far out over the open stairway as she could. The flame flickered in the dank draft wafting up from the coal cellar.

They'd been preparing all day for the supper party Dr. Waterton had planned for Saturday night to celebrate Jack's sixteenth birthday. Mrs. Butters had said there would be twenty-two guests, friends of the family along with some of Jack's friends from school.

The monstrous range in the kitchen consumed every scrap of coal Forrest brought in, and then demanded more. But now Forrest was out and Mrs. Butters had sent Meredith to fill the coal scuttle.

Why did the electric light in the cellar have to burn out the very first time she was sent for coal? There were sure to be spiders and mice—or worse—in the inky darkness. Meredith shuddered. She placed a tentative foot on the first step and listened for the sound of scurrying feet from below. She moved to the second step, then the third, one hand shielding the candle flame as her ears tried to make sense of the darkness.

The hinge on the back door screeched. Meredith scrambled back to the top of the stairs, her heart hammering.

"Hello, there!" The freckled face of the boy holding the back door open looked familiar. "Why, you're the girl with the suitcase!"

"I dropped the candle!" Meredith stared at her empty hand in horror. A burning candle was dangerous.

"I'll get it!" The boy ran across the floor and disappeared down the stairs. "I can't see a thing," he called up to her, "but at least that means it's gone out." His head reappeared at the top of the stairs, and he winked. "No harm done."

The shoeshine boy! Meredith flushed with embarrassment. "It seems you're always getting me out of messes," she said.

"It seems you're always getting into them." Even his freckles seemed to be grinning at her as he climbed the stairs, and this time Meredith found herself smiling back.

"Is Mrs. Butters in?" The boy snatched his cap off and tried unsuccessfully to smooth his curly, red hair.

"She's in the kitchen. How do you know Mrs. Butters?"

"My mam comes to clean."

"Mrs. O'Hagan?" Meredith enjoyed that cheerful lady's stories about her five lively children. "You must be Tommy."

"Thomas Aloysius O'Hagan, if you please," he said. "What did Mam tell you?"

"Only that there were three boys and two girls."

"Paddy and Mick are overseas. Mary's thirteen—a year younger than me—and Bernie's six. You must be the new girl."

"Meredith Hollings, from Port Stuart." Meredith held out her hand.

Tommy took her hand and pumped it up and down enthusiastically. "Pleased to meet you, Miss Hollings. I hope you will allow me to show you the sights of Toronto. When are you free?"

Exploring the city with Tommy might be fun. "On Sunday."

"Sunday, then, but after Mass, or Mam will tan my hide. What would you like to do?"

She realized Tommy still had hold of her hand, so she withdrew it quickly. "Could we ride the streetcar?" She'd loved Papa's stories about the streetcars in Toronto, but then she realized Tommy must be used to riding streetcars. He might think that was childish.

"What's this about Sunday and streetcars?" The hinge on the back door screeched again as Forrest came in, bringing a gust of chilly air in with him. He wiped his feet on the mat, eying Meredith sternly. "Don't you be taking after Alice, young Meredith. She liked gadding about with the soldiers home on leave. Mrs. Butters would have something to say about that, I can tell you."

Meredith hardly knew where to look. What would Tommy think? Eager to escape, she picked up the coal scuttle to start downstairs again, but the yawning dark below made her hesitate.

Forrest's eyebrows were fierce as he frowned at her. "And just what are you doing with that scuttle?"

"Mrs. Butters sent me for coal."

"So you're taking over my job, now? Next thing I know, you'll be driving the car. Well, there's no need for a slip of a girl to be hauling coal." He lifted the empty scuttle out of Meredith's hands and disappeared down the stairs.

"Switch on the light, lassie," he called. "It's dark as the devil down here."

"It's burnt out," Meredith called back. She heard him curse by way of reply.

"I didn't mean to make him angry," she whispered to Tommy. Would Forrest complain about her to Mrs. Butters? Or Parker?

Tommy laughed. "He was just having fun."

"He was joking?" Meredith could have sworn he was cross.

Forrest reappeared with the heaped scuttle.

"Thank you," Meredith said, reaching for it. "I'm not too fond of cellars, especially dark ones."

"I'm not fond of them myself," Forrest said. "I'll take this in, and then I'll have a word with Mrs. Butters. Sending a skinny miss like you for coal!" He certainly sounded grumpy, but now Meredith could see the twinkle in his eye.

They followed Forrest to the kitchen where soup simmering on the back of the range sent out a comforting aroma of beef and onions. He shoveled coal into the firebox of the range, and then settled into his chair at the far end of the table. He nodded at Mrs. Butters before opening the newspaper and disappearing behind it.

Mrs. Butters was rolling out pastry at the other end of the table, her sleeves pushed up to her elbows, her forearms dusty with flour. "Shouldn't you be at work, Tommy O'Hagan?"

Mrs. Butters sounded stern, but she was smiling. It seemed everyone smiled at Tommy. "You can't expect your poor mother to work to feed you all while you're out gallivanting."

"Bernie's sick," Tommy said. "The school sent her home. Mary thinks Mam should come, too."

"Oh, that's a shame. Bernadette seemed fine when she was here the other day," Mrs. Butters said.

Forrest looked up from the paper. "That redheaded imp who played tag with young Harry? The two of them were running around the yard, shrieking like wild things."

Bernadette had clung to her mother when she first caught sight of Meredith, but Harry had soon coaxed her to play with him, much to Meredith's relief. It had given her time to finish cutting up the stewing beef for the consommé Mrs. Butters had planned for the party.

"That's the one. She's caught a cold, like as not. October is terrible for colds." Mrs. Butters folded a thin circle of pastry over the rolling pin and transferred it quickly to the waiting pie plate. "But I was counting on your mother to finish the silver for the party tomorrow."

"Mary says Bernie's forehead is burning up, and Bernie says her head hurts," Tommy said.

"I hope it's not that Spanish Flu they're talking about." Mrs. Butters reached for a bowl piled high with sliced and sugared apples. She poured the apples into the waiting pie plate and covered it with another circle of pastry. "Meredith, you go tell Mrs. O'Hagan she's wanted at home, and then you finish up the silver. Cabbagetown's not far, she'll be home soon enough."

Ragged ribbons of pastry curled onto the table as Mrs. Butters ran a knife around the edge of the pan. "I'll get some bran for a poultice, and onions. Hot bran and onion tea are the best things for a cold." She wiped her hands on her apron before heading to the pantry.

Meredith turned to Tommy. "I hope your sister feels better soon."

"Me, too. But it won't spoil our plans for Sunday—if you still want to go." He looked at her, eyebrows raised.

"Oh, yes! I'm looking forward to it."

Meredith realized Forrest was watching them over the top of the newspaper. She crossed the kitchen quickly and pushed the swinging door so hard it whacked against the wall. She could hear Forrest laughing as she sped along the passageway to the dining room. She hoped Tommy hadn't seen her blushing.

A neat army of gleaming silver stood at one end of the dining room table, a shabby detachment of tarnished pieces at the other. Mrs. O'Hagan sat in the middle, newspaper and rags on the table in front of her, polishing a large platter.

"Tommy's here, Mrs. O'Hagan," Meredith said. "Bernadette's sick. She was sent home from school. Mrs. Butters says you're to go home."

Mrs. O'Hagan looked up. "Bernie was fine this morning. And I haven't finished the silver yet." She inspected the gleaming platter and added it to the shiny battalion.

"I'm to finish it," Meredith said.

"Thank you, dearie." Mrs. O'Hagan rolled down the sleeves of her faded, blue dress and reached behind to untie her large apron. She smoothed her hair—a frizz of orange, not Tommy's startling red—and sighed. "I hate to saddle you with it, but if Bernie's sick, well, there's nothing to be done, is there?" She patted Meredith's arm and headed for the kitchen.

Meredith settled into the vacant chair. It felt warm all up and down her back like a hug from Mama. She chose a small, blackened bowl and dipped a rag into the jar of polishing cream. She wondered what Mama was doing right this minute, and whether Ellen missed her. She scrubbed at the bowl as if she could rub homesickness off along with the tarnish.

She should count her blessings instead of getting all weepy.

One: Mrs. Butters was a dear. She always thanked Meredith for helping.

Two: Harry was getting easier to manage now that she knew his favorite hiding places.

Three: She had plenty to eat, more than she'd had in a long time, because the Watertons didn't need to scrimp.

Meredith set the now-gleaming bowl down, and picked up a serving spoon. The curlicues on its handle would take some work. She whistled as she rubbed in the cream.

Papa had taught her to whistle—"sweet as a nightingale," he'd said—but Mama had disapproved. "A whistling girl and a crowing hen," Mama would caution, "always come to no good end."

So whistling became Meredith's secret, and Papa's. They held whistling contests when Mama and Ellen weren't around.

"Four: I can whistle all I want to in Toronto," she told her upside-down reflection in the bowl of the spoon. But that blessing was bittersweet: she'd rather have Mama nearby and run the risk of a scolding.

She wondered if Tommy liked whistling, too. Only two days until Sunday!

CHAPTER 9

Meredith selected a potato from the pile on the counter and stuck her tongue out at it. She had to be the best potato peeler in Toronto by now. She'd certainly had lots of practice. It was Saturday at last and there was so much to do before the party that evening that she hadn't sat down since her hasty breakfast.

"When you've finished those potatoes, Parker will want you in the dining room to help with the table." Mrs. Butters' cheeks were bright red as she whisked egg whites in a big copper bowl.

"Not just yet, Mrs. Butters," Parker said from the door to the hallway. His voice was thin, his face pale. "I'm going upstairs to lie down for a bit."

Mrs. Butters stopped whisking and looked up at him.

"Not one of your sick headaches?"

Parker nodded, wincing as his head moved.

Mrs. Butters frowned. "Nothing to be done, I suppose?"

Parker shook his head. He winced again.

Mrs. Butters sighed. "I suppose if you get some rest now, you might feel better for the party this evening. Heaven knows we'll need you then."

Parker nodded. Meredith thought he looked shrunken in on himself as he started up the back stairs.

"Mind you put a cool cloth on your forehead," Mrs. Butters called after him. "I'll send Meredith up later with some tea if I can spare her."

Meredith rinsed her freshly peeled potato and added it to the others in the large pot on the counter in front of her. She was sorry Parker's head hurt him—sorry in a Sunday school way, like being sorry for starving people in foreign places—but she wasn't sorry that Parker would be out of their way for a few hours. Although, she supposed glumly, he'd probably pick at her more than ever when he reappeared.

"One of his sick headaches, and today of all days!" Mrs. Butters attacked the egg whites again, the whisk hammering against the bowl this time. "I was going to ask him to go to Galligan's for vanilla. And Forrest won't be back until this afternoon."

"Could I go?" Meredith asked eagerly. She'd done

nothing but wash and peel and chop all morning. It would be heaven to fill her lungs with fresh air.

"I suppose you'll have to." Mrs. Butters sighed. "I just don't know how we are going to get everything ready. Although Mrs. O'Hagan can help with the table when she comes. She should be along any minute."

She set the whisk down and wiped her hands on her apron. "I'll just see if we need anything else," she muttered as she crossed the kitchen to the pantry.

There was a knock at the back door. Meredith wiped her hands and hurried to open it. Her heart did a little skip of pleasure when she discovered Tommy. His face lit up when he saw her.

"Is your sister still sick?" Meredith asked. A gust of crisp air swept into the back hall through the open door.

"Really sick." Tommy wiped his feet on the mat and followed her into the kitchen. "And now Mam's poorly, too. She sent me to say she can't come today."

"Who can't come today?" Mrs. Butters bustled in, her hands on her hips. "Oh, Tommy, no! I was counting on your mother. And now with Parker…what in heaven's name are we going to do?"

"Do you still want me to go to the store?" Meredith asked, fingers crossed.

"Bless you, child, I don't see how I can spare you now. Mr. Harry will be clattering through here any minute."

All the shine went out of the morning for Meredith. It had been her one chance to get out.

"But I can't finish the cake without it," Mrs. Butters went on, throwing her hands in the air, "so someone's got to go. Tommy, could you maybe run to Galligan's for me?"

"I wish I could," Tommy said, "but I can't make it there and back and still get to work on time. Crawley said I'd lose my place if I'm late again."

"Let me do it, Mrs. Butters," Meredith said eagerly. "Please? I'll run the whole way there and back, I promise, and I'll work twice as fast after."

Mrs. Butters sighed. "What choice do I have? Tommy can show you the way, at least. Mind you pay attention so you can find your way back." She took a small, blue tin from the top drawer of the kitchen dresser and counted out some coins. "This should be enough. Mind you ask for the small bottle."

"I will." Meredith slid the coins into the pocket of her skirt. "I'll be back before you know it."

"And here's a penny for you, and one for Tommy for his trouble." Mrs. Butters smiled as she held out two coins. "Buy yourselves a treat. You're good workers, both of you."

"Thank you!" A whole penny was riches. At home, Meredith's mouth always watered when she measured out sweets for those with a penny to spend on candy, but she'd rarely been allowed to have any. Every penny had been precious after Papa left.

Mrs. Butters patted Meredith's shoulder. "Take your sweater. Tommy, tell your mother it's all right. She's not to come back until she's feeling better."

"Yes, ma'am." Tommy put his cap on and headed for the back door. Meredith grabbed her sweater from the hook by the door and followed him onto the porch and down the path.

It was better than wonderful to be outside. The sun warmed Meredith's back, and she felt so filled with fizzy air that she was in danger of lifting off the pavement any minute. As they trotted along the street together, scuffing through the brightly colored leaves, she admired the large homes they passed.

The scent of a late-blooming rose drifted by her nose. There were roses in Rosedale, just as she'd thought. She bet Mrs. Stinson didn't know that.

"This isn't what I meant when I said I'd show you the sights," Tommy said, as he panted beside her, "but we can see a lot more of them this way."

"You could start a business," Meredith said. "Tommy's Trotting Tours of Toronto."

"I'd like that," Tommy said. "But you'd have to come and work for me. A pretty tour leader would bring lots of customers."

A pretty tour leader. Meredith hugged that thought close. "Is it much farther?" she asked, between breaths. "I don't want you to be late."

"That's Yonge Street up ahead. Galligan's is just around the corner."

Yonge Street was crowded with black cars tootling past, and delivery wagons lumbering behind work-a-day horses like Uncle Dan's. The barber's red-and-white striped pole across the street looked just like the one on Port Stuart's main street; a handful of men were waiting inside just like back home. Meredith's eyes were drawn to the milliner's next door where richly colored hats perched like exotic birds in the big window. Black, gray, and lavender hats for mourning huddled discreetly in one corner.

Meredith wished she had time to poke about the shops, but Mrs. Butters would fret if she didn't get back quickly. She'd come and explore one Wednesday afternoon instead.

A cheerful bell above the grocer's door announced their arrival. Inside, a jumble of baskets overflowed with fruit and vegetables, and the shelves behind the counter were stacked to the ceiling with boxes, jars and cans. The scent of oiled wood from the floor made Meredith think of Mama, a kerchief over her hair, sweeping the floor from one side of the store to the other at the end of each day.

Meredith's nose tingled from the tang of the pickle barrel and the sharp smell of cheese. Ellen loved to shave slivers off the big wheels of cheese—for the mice, she always said, but Meredith knew which little mouse gobbled it down when Mama wasn't looking.

Mr. Galligan was as pink and plump as the ham that hung from a hook behind his head. As he fetched a small bottle of vanilla, Meredith fingered the penny Mrs. Butters had given her.

"A penny's worth of lemon drops, please," she said when Mr. Galligan handed her the vanilla. "What will you get, Tommy?"

"Licorice whips," he said promptly. "They're Bernie's favorite."

Meredith offered the bag of lemon drops to Tommy, then popped one into her own mouth. The sour-sweet taste made their mouths pucker at the same time and they laughed at the faces they made. Meredith decided to save some and surprise him tomorrow.

Back outside, Tommy pointed her in the direction of Glenwaring. "Can you find your way back all right?"

"Perfectly," Meredith said.

"What about tomorrow? Say after lunch?"

"That will be perfect, too," Meredith said. She liked how his brown eyes crinkled up when he smiled.

She trotted away from the bustle of Yonge Street,

but couldn't resist looking back over her shoulder. Tommy hadn't moved. He waved to her, and she waved back.

Sunday tomorrow, Sunday tomorrow, she sang to herself, the song keeping time with her feet as she ran along the pavement. A party tonight, a day off tomorrow, and a bag full of sweets to share.

Yonge Street was much like the main street in Port Stuart, she thought. Maybe Toronto was nothing more than a collection of small towns all joined together. It didn't seem so big when she thought of it like that. Maybe she'd like living here so much she wouldn't want to go back to Port Stuart. After all, there were bound to be jobs for teachers in Toronto. And maybe Mama and Ellen could join her here.

The thought made her feel warm right down to her toes.

CHAPTER 10

"Stand still, Meredith, or you'll get jabbed."

Meredith stood stiffly on a chair in the middle of the kitchen. She held her arms away from her sides while Mrs. Butters pinned tucks in the shiny, black fabric at her waist. Alice had been small and plump, so the maid's uniform was far too short and much too wide for Meredith. At lunchtime, Mrs. Butters had shown Meredith how to pick out the hem to let the skirt down. Now that it was nearly time for the party, Mrs. Butters was trying to gather the bodice so Meredith would look respectable.

"That will have to do," Mrs. Butters said at last. "The apron will hide the pins."

Meredith hopped down from the chair and stretched.

"Mind you, those pins won't hold if you jump about

like that," Mrs. Butters said. "Now you go and see Parker. He'll have instructions for you." She sank into the chair that Meredith had hopped off and wiped her forehead.

The bunched fabric at Meredith's waist wasn't at all comfortable, but the taffeta of the full skirt rustled deliciously when she moved. She gently lifted a lacy apron from the kitchen table and carefully tied the strings around her waist so they wouldn't snag on the pins.

"This is like an angel's wing," Meredith fingered the delicate apron, "but it won't do much to keep me clean." She twirled, enjoying the swish of her swirling skirt. She was sure she'd look positively elegant when she pinned the lacy cap on her hair. If only Ellen could see her now!

Meredith caught sight of Mrs. Butters' face and stopped twirling. The cook's eyes were closed, and there was a sheen of sweat across her forehead. Her skin looked gray, as if every line in her face was etched in pencil.

"Mrs. Butters, are you all right?"

Mrs. Butters stirred, blinked, and then mopped at her face with her apron. "I felt a bit faint just now. It must be the heat. I'll just sit for a minute and catch my breath." She reached up and tucked a stray curl behind Meredith's ear. "You go see what Parker needs."

"I'll make you some tea first," Meredith said. She took the canister from the dresser and spooned tea into the teapot, then filled the teapot from the kettle simmering on the range. She fetched a scone from the breadbox and put it on one of the thick, white kitchen plates along with a knife and a small pot of strawberry jam. She set the plate on the table beside Mrs. Butters, who was fanning her face with her apron.

"You should eat something, too," Meredith said. "You've been working hard, but everything's ready so there's nothing for you to do right this minute." She poured tea into one of the cups with the yellow roses and carried it to the table.

"You're a good girl, Meredith." Mrs. Butters reached for the cup. "Take that tray in to Parker now, please. It's nearly six." She sipped the tea and Meredith was relieved to see she looked a little better.

Meredith pinned the wisp of a cap to her dark hair, then curtsied and pulled a silly face that made Mrs. Butters smile. She covered the tray of savories and sandwiches with a linen napkin, hoping there'd be some left at the end of the evening. She'd been chopping and peeling all afternoon while Mrs. Butters created her tiny masterpieces, and she hadn't dared sneak a taste.

She carried the tray carefully across the front hall. With twenty-two guests expected any moment, she didn't know what they'd do if Mrs. Butters took sick, especially as Parker still felt unwell.

She found Parker in one corner of the drawing room

arranging bottles and glasses on a table inlaid with mother-of-pearl. She gently set the tray on a small, wooden table near the piano, careful to not disturb the napkin so the food would stay fresh.

Meredith loved the drawing room. It shone pale-blue and gold like a jewelry box. Graceful chairs in blue-and-cream-striped silk clustered together like ladies taking tea. Elaborate gold, velvet draperies swathed the large windows that lined two sides of the room. Tall mirrors in fanciful gilded frames reflected the early evening light from the windows.

She trailed her fingers across the striped satin of the sofa, thinking it would be wonderful to sit and read all day in this beautiful room. Someday she'd have her own little house, and she'd paint the parlor blue and gold just like this.

"There's no time for daydreaming, girl." Parker looked more severe than usual in his starched white shirt, striped vest, and trim black coat. He was clearly out of sorts.

"Are you feeling better?" Meredith asked. If she was nice and polite, maybe he wouldn't be quite so prickly with her.

"Better enough, I suppose." Parker pressed his mouth into a thin line. "Now listen carefully. When the doorbell rings, I shall open the door for our guests. You are to take their coats to the library while I show them to the drawing room. When all of the guests have arrived, you are to circulate among them and offer the tray. Can you manage that?" Parker's eyes narrowed as if he wasn't sure she could. Meredith nodded eagerly.

"You are not to chat with the guests," he said. "Just a simple 'sir' or 'madam' will suffice when you offer the tray." Parker took a small gold watch from the front pocket of his vest. "And for heaven's sake, don't drop anything." His eyes bored into Meredith. "I am not sure you are quite ready for this."

Meredith sighed. If only he'd stop picking on her! She'd been serious and responsible ever since she'd arrived. She vowed that tonight, she'd be the very best maid he'd ever seen.

Dr. Waterton entered the drawing room, holding Harry by the hand. Harry was pulling at the stiff collar of his white shirt, his wet hair still showing the marks where a comb had slicked it back. When Meredith had been sent to help Harry get ready earlier, he'd complained about the scratchy collar and refused outright to get changed at all. She'd been forced to leave him wearing his play clothes. Meredith wondered what the doctor had said to persuade Harry to wear the hated shirt.

Jack and Maggie followed, arguing hotly. Jack looked suddenly grown up in evening dress, although his bowtie sat slightly askew and his knobby wrists dangled comically from the sleeves of the smart black jacket. Maggie's dress was the cheerful blue of forget-me-nots, covered with all the frills and flounces Ellen pined for. Beside Maggie's splendor, Meredith's black taffeta uniform seemed cheap and shabby.

Meredith was glad to see Jack arguing with his sister. He'd stayed away from her since the evening on the steps, but she was worried that if he decided to tease her here in front of everyone, she'd be in for another lecture from Parker. "There's no place in service for someone who doesn't know her place," Parker had scolded her after he'd seen her talking to Jack on the back step. He hadn't understood she didn't want Jack's attention.

"Father said you're to keep an eye on Harry." Jack scowled at Maggie.

"But it's always me! I don't see why you can't take a turn!"

"It's not always you!" Jack protested. "And it's my party, for heaven's sake!"

"That's enough, you two!" Dr. Waterton let go of Harry's hand. "Maggie, you're to keep an eye on Harry, and I don't want to hear any more about it."

"Oh, all right," Maggie muttered. She threw a sour glance at her little brother as he edged away.

Dr. Waterton sighed. "What time is it, Parker, please?"

"Six-o-clock, sir," Parker said. "May I offer you some sherry?"

"Yes, thank you," the doctor replied.

"Many happy returns, young sir," Parker went on, with a small bow to Jack, who shrugged.

Parker's nostrils flared and his eyes narrowed. Jack's rudeness hadn't improved Parker's mood, which was already well past sour. Meredith knew she'd need to be extra careful not to do anything that might set Parker off.

"Don't stand about gawking," Parker whispered to her, as if he'd heard precisely what she'd been thinking. "Set out more napkins, and keep Mr. Harry away from the food."

"Sixteen years old and already taller than me." Dr. Waterton draped an arm across Jack's shoulders. "You'll make a fine doctor in a few years, son."

Jack moved out from under his father's arm. "I'm going to be a pilot." Meredith remembered how certain he'd sounded on the back step when he talked about flying.

"It seems glamorous just now because of the war, but flying's a hobby, not a career," the doctor said. "There's no future in it."

"It's my birthday!" Jack exclaimed. "And I don't want to talk about that in front of my friends. Can't you just leave it alone for one night?"

Dr. Waterton sighed. "I only want the best for you, Jack, and I know your mother would, too, if she were here."

"You don't know the first thing about it! Mama

wouldn't have minded what I want to do—" Jack began hotly.

"But I'll leave it alone, for now," Dr. Waterton said, talking over him, "since you're not inclined to listen to anything I say."

He turned to Maggie. "How very pretty you look tonight, Maggie."

Maggie ignored the compliment, her face stormy. "It's not fair. Why can't I have a dinner party for my birthday?"

"When you're sixteen," Dr. Waterton said, sounding tired, "you may have a dinner party, too. In the meantime, you've a new dress—a very expensive one, I might add—for this one. And one for which you don't seem the least bit grateful."

The doctor turned to accept a glass of sherry from Parker, so he didn't see Maggie screw up her face and stick out her tongue behind his back. But Maggie caught Meredith watching. For a moment, Meredith thought Maggie might say something to put her in her place, but the other girl turned away.

"Stay away from that tray, Harry!" Maggie said sharply as Harry sidled past the piano. "That food's not for you."

Harry darted a glance at Meredith. She hoped he wasn't going to cause a fuss, not with Parker already in a foul mood. But then the doorbell sounded, Parker beckoned to her, and she hurried after him excitedly. The party was beginning at last.

The whoosh of cold air when Parker opened the big front door made Meredith thankful for the fire warming the entrance hall. A stout, red-faced man handed Meredith his hat and coat. Parker helped a faded-looking woman out of a brown cloth coat that sported a fox collar. At least, Meredith thought it was fox, but the glassy eyes and dangling paws gave her a creepy feeling, so she folded the coat with the creature inside to keep the collar from staring at her.

Meredith carried the coats and the man's hat to the library across the hall. Whenever she had a reason to be in the library, she wanted to read her way up and down the floor-to-ceiling bookshelves from one side of the doorway all the way around the room to the other side. She ran her finger along a row of rich leather bindings. *Great Expectations. Oliver Twist.* She was wondering, not for the first time, if she could ask permission to take a book up to her room, when the sound of the doorbell reminded her she'd better keep her mind on her work.

A flurry of arrivals kept Meredith busy scurrying between the front door and the library. The adults nodded to her politely, but Jack's friends mostly shoved their coats at her and rushed off noisily. When she returned to the drawing room at last, Jack was laughing with his cronies and didn't notice when she slipped past him to get the tray of sandwiches beside the piano. When she removed the linen napkin, she discovered that an entire row of sandwiches had disappeared.

"Oh, Harry!" Maggie crowed from where she stood at the edge of the jostling group surrounding Jack. "You're in trouble now!"

"Mr. Harry! Those were for the guests!" Meredith scolded.

Harry scooted out from behind the piano, furiously chewing. Dr. Waterton made a grab for him as the doorbell sounded again.

"Any more of that, young man, and you'll be sent upstairs," he said. Harry hung his head.

Dr. Waterton turned to Meredith. "Please have Mrs. Butters replenish the tray," he said. "Jack, you go and greet your guests and help Parker with the coats. Maggie, you are to keep tight hold of Harry's hand."

Meredith quickly carried the half-empty tray to the kitchen. "Mrs. Butters," she called as she pushed the door open, "we need more sandwiches."

The pan of consommé simmered on the range, but the sharp odor of vinegar cut through the rich beef-and-wine aroma and undercut the smell of roasting turkey. A huge pot of potatoes—forty-two potatoes, who would believe it?—was bubbling merrily beside the soup. Other pots sat on the counter, filled with the vegetables Meredith had prepared earlier. Silver baskets were lined up on the counter like beds in a dormitory, white linen napkins tucked tidily around the rolls to keep them fresh. Two enormous glass bowls of lettuce and cucumber waited for Mrs. Butters' special vinaigrette, but there was no sign of her.

A faint noise came from the pantry. Meredith set the tray down and hurried to investigate.

Mrs. Butters lay like a jumble of laundry on the stone floor of the pantry. Shards of crockery explained the acrid smell and the dark wetness spreading across the floor.

"Mrs. Butters! What happened?" Meredith held her skirt up to keep it out of the vinegar and knelt beside her. She reached a tentative hand toward the cook's shoulder. "Mrs. Butters? What's wrong?"

Mrs. Butters moaned. She was shivering.

"I'll fetch the doctor." Meredith straightened.

"No!" Mrs. Butters' voice was faint, but clear. "Help me up."

Meredith hesitated. "You need a doctor."

Mrs. Butters shook her head.

"All right, then." Meredith positioned herself behind Mrs. Butters, then slipped her arms under the cook's shoulders and pulled. Mrs. Butters moaned and her weight shifted slightly, but Meredith wasn't strong enough to pull her to her feet.

"Don't worry. I'll try from the front." Meredith picked her way through the mess on the floor, and then decided she should clear away the broken crockery first. She was hastily gathering the jagged pieces, her eyes searching the floor for slivers, when she realized that the broom might be faster. She skirted the wet patch to fetch it.

Spying the half-empty tray on the kitchen table, she realized with horror that she should have returned to the drawing room by now. Parker would be furious with her. But if she went back now, she'd have to stay and serve the guests, and she couldn't leave Mrs. Butters lying here on the floor.

Meredith was standing in the kitchen with the broom in her hand, her thoughts spinning, when the door from the hall swung open and banged hard against the kitchen wall.

"Papa says, 'Hurry up.'" Maggie stood inspecting the kitchen, her hands on her hips. She wrinkled her nose. "It stinks in here."

"Mrs. Butters is sick. A crock broke in the pantry. I'm cleaning it up." The words tumbled out in Meredith's haste to explain. "I need your help."

"Help with what?" Maggie frowned. "I'm not going to clean anything up, if that's what you mean."

"With Mrs. Butters," Meredith explained. "She's on the floor in the pantry."

"Really?" Maggie crossed the kitchen and peered into the pantry. She turned to face Meredith. "What do you expect me to do about it?"

"Help me lift her so we can get her out of there."

"Lift her? She's much too heavy for that. Besides, her skirt is soaked. I don't want my dress covered in whatever that is." Maggie made her way to the kitchen table and helped herself to a sandwich from the tray. "Get Forrest."

How could Maggie Waterton stand there calmly eating a sandwich, as if it were perfectly normal to see kind Mrs. Butters lying sick on the floor? "Forrest's not here," Meredith said. "Please, can't you help? Or get Parker, at least?"

Maggie backed away. "Why should I help you?"

"It's not for me; it's for Mrs. Butters."

Mrs. Butters moaned again.

"Please," Meredith begged, "she's so sick."

Maggie let out a tortured sigh. "Oh, all right. I'll see if Parker can come." She popped the last of the tiny sandwich into her mouth and headed for the passageway.

"You'll be all right, Mrs. Butters," Meredith said, stroking the cook's arm gently. "Miss Maggie's gone to get help."

CHAPTER 11

"Hallo!" A cold draft from the back door flooded in a few minutes later. "Where is everyone?"

Relief flooded Meredith. It seemed as if she'd been waiting for hours. "In the pantry!" she called to Forrest. "Hurry!"

"What a smell! What have you done now, young Meredith?" Forrest halted in the doorway. "Hey now, what's all this?" He squatted beside Meredith who was cradling Mrs. Butters' head in her lap.

"She isn't feeling well, she felt faint before, and Dr. Waterton sent me to refill the tray, and I found her like this, and I couldn't move her, and I'm..." Meredith's voice faltered, a hot prickle behind her eyes.

"First things first," said Forrest. "Let's sit her up."

He slid his arms under the cook's shoulders and eased her to a sitting position. He peered into her face. "What's wrong, Elvie?"

Mrs. Butters sagged against him like a scarecrow Meredith had seen from the train, its limbs and head at impossible angles after a summer's worth of wind and rain.

Forrest laid his hand on Mrs. Butters' forehead. "She's burning up."

The cook's face looked dragged down. Her eyelids fluttered, and then her eyes rolled back and her mouth fell open. Meredith couldn't bear to look.

"This is a right mess," Forrest said. "I don't like the looks of her. Does the doctor know?"

Meredith shook her head. "She wouldn't let me fetch him, but Miss Maggie's getting Parker."

"Maggie?" His eyebrows shot up. "How did you manage that?"

"Dr. Waterton sent her to the kitchen to see why it was taking so long to fill the tray. She wouldn't help me lift Mrs. Butters, but she said she'd tell Parker."

Forrest snorted. "I wouldn't count on it. The boys are fond of Mrs. Butters, but that chit cares only about herself."

The dim light from the electric bulb overhead colored Mrs. Butters' face the hopeless gray of dishwater. Meredith asked herself how Mrs. Butters could be this sick. How could it have happened so fast?

"Let's see if we can get her to the settee in the back hall. She'd be more comfortable there," Forrest suggested.

"Elvie?" he said loudly. "Can you stand up?"

Mrs. Butters' head lolled against his chest, but her eyes opened and she shook her head.

Forrest sighed. "We'll have to carry her, lassie. I'll take her shoulders; you take her feet."

Meredith nodded. She got into position and grasped the cook's ankles. "Ready."

"On three: one, two, three!" Forrest grunted as he struggled to his feet. Meredith staggered as they lifted the dead weight, and then Mrs. Butters' ankles slipped from Meredith's grasp. Mrs. Butters cried out as her heels slammed against the floor.

"Oh, Mrs. Butters! I'm sorry! I didn't mean to!" Meredith's hands flew to her mouth.

"Steady now," Forrest said. "We'll try it again."

"But what if I hurt her?" Meredith's feet were welded to the floor.

"Meredith, lass, she's too heavy for me on my own." Forrest's face was crimson and he was sweating. "You'll manage it this time," he said, panting. "Come on now, give it a go."

Meredith took hold of Mrs. Butters' ankles once more, then quickly straightened up.

"There we are!" Forrest beamed at her. "All right, lass?"

Meredith nodded.

"I'll go first. You tell me if I've got a clear road." Forrest backed out of the pantry. The cook's wet skirt slid partway up her legs, but there was no time to worry about modesty. Meredith tried to match the rhythm of Forrest's steps as they trekked across the kitchen, a trail of vinegar footprints marking their unsteady progress. She willed herself to ignore the strain in her arms, but they were trembling by the time they reached the back hall.

"Easy now," Forrest said as they lowered Mrs. Butters to the settee, but Meredith's cramped fingers let go all at once and Mrs. Butters' feet thumped onto the taut horsehair seat.

Meredith rubbed her aching arms as Forrest took a coat from the rack, folded it and then slipped it under Mrs. Butters' head. He covered her with another coat.

"That's all we can do for now, lassie. We'll have the doctor look in on her later. You'd best go back to the party."

"But there's the dinner to finish!"

"I may not look it, but I know a thing or two about cooking," Forrest said. "If I could fight the Boers, I guess I can serve a dinner. Tell Parker—discreetly, mind—that dinner might be somewhat delayed." Forrest laid a hand on her arm. "And don't fret. We've a doctor in the house, remember?" He winked.

Forrest was right, of course. Meredith felt much better as she refilled the sandwich tray.

CHAPTER 12

When she returned to the party, Meredith discovered Forrest had been right about something else: Maggie hadn't said a word to Parker.

Parker's eyes widened when Meredith whispered that Mrs. Butters was ill. "No need to tell the family," was all he said after she assured him that she and Forrest could carry out the final preparations for dinner.

Parker's nose quivered as he said it, and he drew back from her a little. Then, when the guests sniffed the air as she passed by, Meredith was certain she reeked of vinegar. It couldn't be helped, so she tried not to mind, even when Jack's friends made a rowdy show of holding their breath. Maggie ignored her altogether, but Meredith knew that had nothing to do with the vinegar.

For Meredith, the evening spun crazily among three worlds. In the dining room, silver candelabra stood guard over the long table set with gold-rimmed china, cut crystal and gleaming cutlery. The candlelight cast a warm glow on the women in silks and velvets, the men in evening dress, and Jack's friends looking uncomfortably tucked in and tidy. The snippets of talk Meredith overheard while shuttling to and from the kitchen mainly concerned the war and the latest show at Shea's Palace on Yonge Street.

"Your cook is a gem, John," an elderly lady in purple silk remarked as Parker signaled Meredith to begin clearing the soup plates. An appreciative murmur went around the table. Meredith glanced at Maggie, who lifted her chin and looked away. Meredith pictured dropping a soup spoon on Maggie's head, but she knew Parker would never believe it was an accident.

The second world consisted of the maelstrom raging in the kitchen. Oven doors banged, pot lids clanged, knives flashed, and spoons clattered as Forrest stirred and carved and served up onto waiting platters as if he'd grown eight arms. His face was the deep red of Mrs. Butters' cranberry relish and he sported a blob of mashed potato above his left eye.

Meredith journeyed between those two worlds. She cleared plates, brought fresh ones, replenished platters, and relayed messages from Parker to Forrest and back again.

Each time she entered the dining room she mirrored Parker's bland expression so that no one would suspect their food was being dished up by a retired soldier who cursed the big, black range in some language he must have picked up in South Africa.

The third world, the one that pulled at her relentlessly as if she were its moon, was the dreary back hall. Meredith checked on Mrs. Butters whenever she could spare a moment. In the lull after the main course had been cleared and the salad had been served, she offered Mrs. Butters some water, but the cook only mumbled and shifted on the makeshift bed.

"Leave her be, lass," Forrest said wearily. "We'll have the doctor look in when the party's over. It won't be long now. There's only dessert and coffee left." He pushed his damp hair back from his forehead, and then peered at the white goo on his fingers.

"It's potato," Meredith said.

Forrest had such a comical look on his face that Meredith giggled, and soon they were both laughing.

"Potato!" croaked Forrest, bent double, his hand smacking the counter.

"Potato!" gasped Meredith, her sides hurting from laughing so hard. And then suddenly she was crying, missing Mama desperately, wishing someone would help kind Mrs. Butters.

"Hey now, lassie." Forrest patted her shoulder. "Don't get yourself in a state. It'll be all right."

Meredith struggled to catch her breath. She swiped the silly apron across her eyes. It was more handkerchief than apron anyway.

"It's been a long day," Forrest said, "but we'll soon be finished. You'd best get back to the dining room. Parker will want help to clear the salad plates."

Meredith nodded. She didn't trust her voice to squeeze around the lump in her throat that had nothing to do with mashed potato. She pasted on a watery smile. As she headed back to the dining room carrying a tray, she wondered if she could find some excuse to ask Dr. Waterton to come to the kitchen, but her head throbbed from crying and she couldn't think how to manage it.

"What about this Spanish Flu business, John?" A woman in taupe looked expectantly at Dr. Waterton as Meredith entered the dining room. "Do you think it will spread into the city?"

Conversation stopped. Meredith stole a glance at Dr. Waterton, who was running his finger around the rim of his wine glass.

Parker motioned for Meredith to begin clearing the salad plates. Worry over Mrs. Butters made her hands tremble, but she was careful not to bang the plates together so she wouldn't call attention to herself.

"I, for one, do not," declared an important-looking man whose high color made Meredith think his shirt collar was buttoned too tightly. "Soldiers are naturally more susceptible—they've been weakened by fighting, after all. But there's no reason for healthy citizens to be alarmed."

There were scattered murmurs of assent.

"It's early days yet," Dr. Waterton said finally, "but we're taking precautions, of course." He nodded at Meredith as she removed his plate. "If people are sensible, there's no immediate danger."

"The Medical Officer—McCready, is it?—says it's no epidemic," said a man seated beside Maggie. Meredith removed his plate quickly so she'd stay clear of Maggie.

"It's those Germans!" A matron upholstered in green velvet turned to her neighbor. "They say the German army puts the flu germs in their bombs."

The guests at Dr. Waterton's end of the table began arguing their own theories, while Jack's mates clamored about their eagerness to sign up for military duty before the war ended. Meredith cleared the last of the plates while Parker used a silver-handled brush to sweep crumbs off the tablecloth into a little, silver crumb tray.

The smells from the ladies' perfumes, the wine and the burning candles made Meredith's head ache. She could almost sympathize with Parker, who looked as if his head was still paining him. Even though her tray was almost too heavy to carry, she was thankful to escape the stuffy dining room. Once in the kitchen, she unloaded the tray, collected the dessert plates and the silver cake knife, and headed back to the dining room. Nearly over, thank heavens.

As Meredith set the plates and the cake knife in front of Jack, she felt a tug on her skirt. Her cheeks burned, but anger quickly replaced embarrassment. He wasn't so grown-up if he played some ridiculous game to annoy her while she was working. She'd be the one reprimanded if she dropped a stack of plates because of his silly notions. He was just like his sister, caring only for himself. Meredith fumed as she waited beside the door for Parker to bring in the dessert.

A tap on the door alerted her. She swung the door open and every head swiveled to watch Parker carry in an enormous cake with candles that lit his face from below. Extravagant whorls of creamy white frosting were dotted with the yellow rosettes Mrs. Butters had painstakingly fashioned. Meredith wished she could pluck one of those delicious-looking rosettes and pop it into her mouth. She'd been so busy she'd forgotten all about eating the snack Mrs. Butters had left ready for her.

A relieved "Ah!" rose from the guests as Parker set the cake in front of Jack, who made a great show of closing his eyes and blowing out the candles to general applause and cheers from his friends.

"First slice for Harry!" Jack said. He sawed off an enormous piece and clumsily slid it onto a plate to a round of laughter. He handed the plate to Meredith and then licked the icing off his fingers as she carried the plate around the table.

"Where is Harry?" Dr. Waterton asked. The chair beside Maggie was empty. "When did he disappear, Maggie?"

Maggie shrugged.

"He's likely in the kitchen with Mrs. Butters," Jack said.

Meredith knew that wasn't possible, and Maggie didn't look as if she was going to try and find her brother. After setting the plate at Harry's place, Meredith eased his chair back and peered underneath the table. A small figure crouched amongst a forest of legs.

"Here he is," Meredith said as she held the tablecloth up. Jack's friends hooted.

"Harry Waterton, come out of there this instant!" Dr. Waterton's tone was all business, but Harry didn't move. Meredith thought he looked pale and drained of energy.

Maggie pushed her chair back. "Come out, Harry. The joke's over," she said, grabbing for his arm.

"I don't feel good," Harry mumbled as he pulled away from her. Meredith could see him shivering.

"You're faking," Maggie said. "You just don't like getting caught."

"Maggie, stop," said Dr. Waterton, who had come around the table. "Harry, I think you ate too many of those sandwiches." He looked down at his youngest son and shook his head. "Jack, you continue with the cake. I'll take Harry upstairs." He gathered Harry into his arms and then frowned as he felt Harry's forehead. "I won't be long," he said to the guests. "Please just carry on without me. Parker will serve the coffee."

He started toward the door carrying Harry, the boy's legs dangling like those of a marionette. "Meredith, you come upstairs with me, please."

Jack patted Harry's leg as the small procession passed him on the way to the hall. "Good night, old fellow," he said gently, surprising Meredith. "We'll save you some cake for tomorrow."

Meredith hurried after the doctor. This was her chance to ask him to check on Mrs. Butters.

CHAPTER 13

Upstairs, Harry balked when Meredith tried to undress him, so Dr. Waterton stripped off the little boy's shirt and trousers and helped him into his flannel nightshirt.

"He's definitely warm," Dr. Waterton said to Meredith, "but I doubt it's serious. I think you should stay here with him and keep him from getting up and running around. If we're lucky, he might just fall asleep."

"Yes, sir."

"I'll be back, Harry," Dr. Waterton said cheerfully. "Be a good boy and stay in bed. Meredith's going to sit here with you."

A hum of voices swirled into the room from downstairs as the doctor opened the bedroom door. He was gone before Meredith could tell him about Mrs. Butters.

The bed springs creaked as Harry sat up. "It's hot in here. Open the window."

"Why don't I take some of these covers off?" Meredith peeled back the blue, quilted bedspread and the white, wool blanket underneath, and folded them carefully over the end of the bed. "I'll leave the sheet so you won't catch a chill. You can pull these up again if you get cold."

"I'm not cold, I'm hot. And I want the window open!"

He's only six, Meredith reminded herself, same as Ellen, and he isn't feeling well. "We'll ask your father about the window when he comes back," she said. "Would you like a drink of water?"

"NO! I want the window open!" Harry's face was a boiled tomato as he thumped the mattress. "You have to do it because I said so!" He began kicking the sheet into a twisted mess. Meredith reached across the bed to take hold of his arms and get him to lie still, but he kicked her, hard, in the stomach.

"You rude little monster!" The words flew out as if Harry had kicked them, too. Meredith doubled over, clutching at her middle. When the pain began to subside, she straightened up gingerly, like a fist unclenching.

Harry lay still. He looked small and ill, and his face, for once, wasn't scowling. "I'm sick," he whispered.

"I know." Meredith reached for his hand. His hot fingers curled around hers. "Let's have a story."

Harry nodded, so Meredith reached for the *Boy's Own Annual* on the table beside the bed. She read until she felt the little fingers loosen their grip, and then she rested her head against the tall back of the rocker and closed her eyes. It was late and she was tired. Port Stuart seemed a thousand miles away.

She startled when the door opened again—minutes or hours later, she couldn't tell—but there was no hum of voices this time. The guests must have left.

"I've brought my bag," Dr. Waterton said, "so let's see what we can do to make Harry better."

"He said he was hot, sir. Can I open the window?"

"Yes, please," the doctor said. "Wake up now, Harry," he said as he shook the little boy awake. Harry blinked up at him like a sleepy turtle.

Dr. Waterton slid a thermometer into Harry's mouth. "Keep that under your tongue and keep your mouth closed. Don't bite on it." He took out his pocket watch, and then felt for Harry's pulse, his eyebrows drawn together.

Meredith tugged on the heavy window sash, and the rush of night air made her long for the breeze off the lake at home. Her eyes wandered across the rooftops and lighted windows of Rosedale.

"You have a fever, Harry. I'll mix some Aspirin powder in water and that should help." Dr. Waterton took a tin and a small spoon from his black bag. He poured water from the carafe on the bedside table into the glass that stood beside it, then spooned in some powder and stirred the mixture vigorously.

Harry's eyes narrowed as he looked at the glass. "My head hurts."

"This will help with that, too," the doctor said. "Sit up straight and drink this down." He patted his son on the back as Harry tentatively sipped the cloudy water.

Harry screwed his face into a tight knot. "It's sour."

"Drink it up anyway." Dr. Waterton tousled his hair. "Meredith will save you a piece of cake to make up for it."

"With roses," Harry said.

"Definitely with roses." The doctor snapped his bag shut and turned to Meredith. "Can you sit with him for a while longer? Just until he falls asleep."

"Yes, sir." This was her chance. Meredith followed him into the hall. "Dr. Waterton, may I speak to you?"

"Are you worried about Harry?" the doctor asked. "He's more than likely caught something at school. Or maybe it really was those sandwiches. Nothing to be alarmed about."

"No, sir. It's not that," Meredith began. "He's not the only one who's sick—"

"Dr. Waterton! Come quickly!" Forrest was rushing along the hallway toward them, his face scarlet and his shirttails sticking out. "It's Mrs. Butters!"

CHAPTER 14

Waiting was agony. Meredith stood at the door of Harry's bedroom, straining to hear something from downstairs, but the house was quiet. She desperately wanted to go down to the kitchen, but she needed to wait until Harry was asleep. She tiptoed over to the bed to check on him again, expecting to see his eyes still wide open, but this time they were closed, the bed covers rising and falling evenly as he slept.

Meredith sped down the back stairs and into the kitchen. Stacks of dirty plates, smudged glasses, and a jumble of pots and pans crowded together on the table and counters. Forrest was leaning against the archway leading to the back hall; Parker stood beside him. Meredith positioned herself behind them and craned her neck to see.

Dr. Waterton had taken off his jacket and rolled up the sleeves of his shirt, despite the cold air streaming in from the open back door. He'd tied his handkerchief over his nose and mouth.

Someone had stacked pillows behind Mrs. Butters so that she was sitting nearly upright, still in her apron with her sleeves pushed up as if she'd just this moment stepped away from the stove. Meredith told herself it was the dim light in the back hall that made Mrs. Butters' skin look so gray. She didn't have an explanation for the faint wheezing sound as Mrs. Butters' chest rose and fell.

The doctor took off his glasses and rubbed his eyes.

"Do you know what it is, sir?" Parker asked. He looked gray, too, in the dim light. Neither he nor Forrest had noticed Meredith arrive.

"She's feverish, but it's the labored breathing I'm worried about," Dr. Waterton said, his voice somewhat muffled by the handkerchief.

"Pneumonia?" Forrest asked.

The doctor nodded. "Most likely."

"But that's highly infectious!" Parker exclaimed. "Are we in any danger?"

"Could…could she die?" Meredith ventured. The three men turned toward her, clearly surprised to find her in the kitchen.

"You've scared the lass," Forrest said, frowning at Parker.

"We've a right to know," Parker said.

"He's not scaring me," Meredith said. "I know about pneumonia. My grandfather died from it."

"We're going to do everything we can to keep that from happening here." Dr. Waterton's calm voice and steady gaze were meant to be reassuring, but Meredith knew what he wasn't saying. No one was safe from pneumonia.

Mrs. Butters stirred. Meredith wondered if she could hear what they said.

"Let's go into the kitchen," the doctor said. "Mrs. Butters needs her rest."

The sudden ringing of the telephone jolted Parker into action. "If you'll excuse me, sir," he said quickly. He scuttled across the kitchen and disappeared through the door to the front hall.

Dr. Waterton sat in the chair at the head of the kitchen table, and pushed the handkerchief off his face and down around his neck. "Sit down, Forrest. You, too, Meredith. Is Harry asleep?"

"Yes, sir." Meredith took the chair beside Forrest. At the other end of the table, a tower of coffee cups tilted precariously over the remains of the cake, where a lone rosette tried its best to look jaunty. The kitchen clock showed it was past eleven, its stately tick-tock measuring the worried silence. Meredith realized Jack and Maggie must have gone to bed.

Forrest cleared his throat. "You think it could be the Spanish Flu," he said. It wasn't a question.

"Could be," Dr. Waterton said.

Forrest swore under his breath. "What do we do?"

"You'll need to wear something over your nose and mouth when you're near her, like this," the doctor said, pointing to the handkerchief. "It might help protect against the germs."

"Might, sir?" Forrest echoed the question in Meredith's mind.

"If it is the Spanish Flu—and it's only an 'if' right now—then it spreads by airborne germs—by coughing or sneezing, for example," the doctor said.

Meredith remembered one of the guests saying the Germans put flu in their bombs. Was that what he meant by germs?

"You should change the mask every two hours," the doctor continued, "and boil it before you use it again to kill any germs."

The door from the hall swung open. "It was the hospital, sir," Parker said. "You're needed."

"Thank you, Parker. Join us, please."

"Of course," Parker said promptly, taking a seat at the table, but his flared nostrils indicated his displeasure.

"I'm explaining about Mrs. Butters," Dr. Waterton said. "Keep the window and door in the back hall open as much as you can. The cold might help bring down her fever, and fresh air should help clear the germs away. Wash your hands after you've touched her."

One, two, three ticks from the kitchen clock. Parker cleared his throat. "If Mrs. Butters is as ill as that," he began, "surely she should be in hospital?"

For once, Meredith agreed with him.

Dr. Waterton looked at Parker over the tops of his glasses. "There's nothing we can do for her there that can't be done here. In fact, she'll likely be better off here with you. It will be quieter, for one thing, so she'll get more rest. If the Spanish Flu spreads across the city, the hospitals—all of them—will be bedlam."

"Then we should send her home," Parker suggested. Two spots of bright color flamed on his cheeks. "She'd be more comfortable in her own bed."

"But there's no one there," Meredith said.

The doctor raised his eyebrows.

"At her house, I mean," Meredith explained. "Mrs. Butters lives alone. Her husband is dead and her son Ben is overseas."

Dr. Waterton nodded. "I can't in good conscience

send her home to an empty house, Parker," he said. "She'll be better here with you."

Parker's eyes grew round. "With me, sir?"

"You, and Meredith," the doctor said with a sigh. "Forrest, too, once I see what the situation is at the hospital."

"I'll help wherever needed, sir, of course," Forrest said. Parker looked as if he'd bitten into a particularly sour crabapple.

"I'll be back," Dr. Waterton said. "You won't be all on your own." He reached into his bag and took out the small tin Meredith had seen him use for Harry.

"Mix this Aspirin powder with water; the directions are on the label," he said, handing the tin to Parker. "Give her sips of plain water as often as you can. Wet her lips if she can't drink. Sponge her face and neck every half hour with a cold, wet cloth to help bring down the fever. Sit her up if she starts to cough, or has trouble breathing. Can you do that?"

Parker's eyes had grown wider with each instruction. Powder, water, sponge, cough, trouble, Meredith repeated the words in her head, like a list for a spelling bee.

"You're certain we're safe?" Parker asked, his fingers worrying a button on his vest.

"Nothing's certain, Parker," Dr. Waterton looked steadily at the butler. "You're healthy, and that's the best thing, but you'll be safer if you take precautions. Can you manage that?"

Parker nodded slowly.

Meredith vowed she'd do her best for Mrs. Butters' sake, and Parker would be there to help, after all. "Yes, sir," she said, hoping her voice didn't sound as shaky as she felt.

"Any idea how she caught it, sir?" asked Forrest. "Elvie hasn't been near the Base Hospital."

"Hard to say just yet. There are suspected cases in Cabbagetown," Dr. Waterton said.

"Mrs. O'Hagan's from Cabbagetown!" Meredith blurted.

"O'Hagan?" Dr. Waterton frowned. "Is that the woman who comes to clean? When was she here last?"

"Hold on," Forrest said. "Wasn't it her little girl running around the garden with Mr. Harry earlier this week?"

"She was last here on Thursday," Meredith said, thinking back. "That was two days ago. She had to leave early because her daughter was sick, and she couldn't come yesterday, or today, either," Meredith was making sense of it in her own mind as she spoke, "Her son came to tell us she was sick."

No one said anything for a moment.

"Let's not jump to conclusions," Dr. Waterton said at last. "I'm going to check on Harry. Parker, help Meredith settle Mrs. Butters here and then come upstairs. Forrest, you get the car."

The doctor crossed the kitchen and disappeared through the door to the hall. Forrest grabbed his coat and headed out the back door.

Dr. Waterton had said not to jump to conclusions, but Meredith's thoughts were whirling. She'd sat in Mrs. O'Hagan's chair. She'd helped carry Mrs. Butters. She'd been sitting with Harry. If any of them had this Spanish Flu, could she get sick, too?

"The doctor's instructions were very clear." Parker's dry voice wrenched her back to the kitchen. "You are to remain here with Mrs. Butters."

"He said both of us."

"I'm afraid you misunderstood. Although I know I shouldn't be surprised at that, since you've had no training." Parker's lizard eyes pinned Meredith to her chair. "Dr. Waterton clearly stated that you are to take care of Mrs. Butters under my supervision."

"That's not what he said—" Meredith began.

"And," Parker ignored her, surveying the cluttered kitchen, "I expect this mess to be cleared up in good time."

"I can't do all that. Not on my own." Meredith hated the waver in her voice. "Can't the cleaning up wait? What if Mr. Harry wakes up?"

"There's no need to let our standards slip. There's no

reason you can't carry out your duties while Mrs. Butters is sleeping." Parker narrowed his eyes. "That is what you are paid for. And in the meantime," he went on, "I shall personally make sure that Mr. Harry has the best possible care."

"But it's been such a long night—"

"There are no 'buts' when I am in charge." Parker stood, brushing at the sleeves of his coat. He looked as crisply tailored as he had at the start of the evening. "I suggest you remember that.

"Unless," he added, "you'd prefer to seek employment elsewhere?"

Meredith wanted to shriek at horrible Parker, but she merely shook her head.

"I thought not," Parker said.

CHAPTER 15

Hours later, Meredith sat slumped at the kitchen table, her head on her arms, too tired to sleep. Sunlight slid across the counter and over the dishes she hadn't had the energy to put away.

She'd sponged Mrs. Butters through the night and worked at clearing up the kitchen in an endless trudge toward morning. Now her bones ached, every one of them as heavy as Mrs. Butters' marble rolling pin. Her shoes seemed two sizes too small for her sore feet. The tea towel she'd been using as a mask sat bunched into a soggy clump around her neck. She longed for smooth, white sheets and the comforting weight of the coverlet to calm her thoughts and take her to a blissful place with no sickness, no dishes—no Parker.

The long hands of the kitchen clock showed six-thirty. It must be Sunday morning. She wondered whether Mrs. Butters would have been busy with breakfast by now.

Meredith sat up and pushed her heavy hair back from her face. The dratted hairpins had come loose again. She shook her hair free, then bundled it into a knot behind her head and jabbed the pins into place.

She replaced the soggy towel around her neck with a fresh one from a drawer in the kitchen dresser. Three were already stewing in the copper boiler on the back of the range. It was all very well for Dr. Waterton to tell them to change their masks every two hours and boil them—he wasn't the one who had to set them to boil, and then rinse them and hang them up to dry.

Meredith filled a small tin basin with cool water and carried it to the back hall. The cold air streaming in hadn't brought Mrs. Butters' fever down yet, but Meredith thought it might be keeping it from getting any higher.

Meredith dipped a cloth in the water, wrung it out, and gently dabbed at the cook's face and neck. Mrs. Butters didn't look any better now that it was morning—her skin was the waxy color of the lilies that had been draped across Granddad's coffin. Meredith stroked the cook's arm gently, wishing she could do more for this woman who had been so kind to her.

She sponged Mrs. Butters for several minutes, and

then set the basin on the floor beside the settee. She stepped out onto the back porch and into the morning sunshine. On the path leading from the porch, pigeons pecked and bobbed, making throaty noises. Crows were arguing in the distance. She could hear the jingle of harness and a friendly *clop-clopping* of a cart horse plodding down a nearby street. The scent of damp earth and dry leaves made her think of the tins of fragrant tobacco she and Ellen stacked into pyramids in the big front window of the store.

A sudden longing for a cup of tea drew Meredith back inside. She paused by the settee to listen to Mrs. Butters' breathing. It sounded raspy, but she couldn't tell if it was worse than before. As she added coal to the range and set the kettle to boil, she prayed the doctor would return soon.

"I see you're awake in good time. What have you done about breakfast?" Parker's voice made Meredith jump. He stood just inside the door from the hall, his bald head pink and shiny, his clean, white shirt making Meredith miserably aware of her limp, creased uniform and the lacy apron spattered with stains.

"Did you hear me, girl? I asked about breakfast." The tip of Parker's beaky nose quivered.

No offer of help, no word of thanks. "Mrs. Butters is sick."

"I know Mrs. Butters is sick," Parker said testily, "but the family will be expecting breakfast."

"There hasn't been time." Meredith lifted her chin. Fair was fair. "I've only just finished the dishes."

"Then you've taken a very long time doing them," Parker said. "I shall most certainly need to think about your suitability for this position."

Meredith's resolve crumbled.

"I suggest you start on breakfast," Parker went on. "Dr. Waterton likes his coffee first thing."

"He's back?" Meredith asked eagerly. They'd be all right now. Even the kitchen looked brighter, somehow.

"No," Parker said, "but it's best to be prepared."

Meredith's heart sank. The long day stretched out endlessly in front of her.

"Bread and jam will do for the children," Parker said. "You can manage that, at least?"

He thinks I'm as stupid as…as *Alice*, Meredith thought, bristling. "Mrs. Butters is sick and all you can think about is bread and jam?"

Parker said nothing at first, but his cold eyes froze her in place. "I am prepared to overlook that unfortunate outburst in light of the difficult night we have all had," he said at last, "but I will not do so a second time."

Don't let anger be your master. Mama's words. Parker could have her fired. He could make sure she wouldn't get another job. Without her wages, Mama might have to sell the store.

Meredith dropped her gaze. There was no use arguing. A wave of tiredness threatened to swamp her as she turned away from Parker and headed for the pantry. Once there, she untied the lacy apron from around her waist and set it aside. She lifted her work apron from its hook and slipped it over the sad-looking, black taffeta uniform.

If I have to make breakfast, Meredith said to herself as she tied the strings behind her back, I'd better look like a cook.

CHAPTER 16

Meredith surveyed the hasty breakfast she'd cobbled together: some cheese, sliced apples, half a loaf of bread, a dish of Mrs. Butters' raspberry jam. The meager offering looked decidedly bedraggled amidst the splendor of the satin walls and gleaming furniture in the dining room. It had been a ridiculous waste of time setting it all out the way Parker insisted. Jack was still sleeping, and Maggie had declared she was too tired to eat. Parker had taken a tray up to Harry but soon brought it back, untouched, because the little boy wasn't hungry.

The telephone sounded while Meredith was loading the dishes onto her tray. She hoped it was the doctor, or Forrest, calling to say they'd be returning soon. Mrs. Butters' raspy breathing was getting worse, and Meredith was sure her fever hadn't come down at all.

"That was Forrest," Parker reported when Meredith reached the kitchen with the laden tray. "He said the doctor will make it home as soon as he can. I asked about a nurse, but he said the hospital couldn't spare any. Forrest himself is staying on to help until the doctor's ready to come home, although I can't think what he could be doing that's so urgent." He pushed his plate away and dabbed at the corners of his mouth.

Meredith set the tray on the counter. Knowing the doctor would be coming eased her worry about Mrs. Butters. She was gloomily contemplating the prospect of washing the dishes when a choking noise erupted in the back hall.

She reached Mrs. Butters' side just as her jagged breathing started up again. Heart pounding, she rearranged the pillows behind Mrs. Butters to prop her more upright.

"Please get better," Meredith whispered, but Mrs. Butters didn't seem to know Meredith was there with her. Meredith laid her cheek against the scratchy wool of the coat draped over the comforting bulk of the cook. Looking after Mrs. Butters, cooking, washing dishes—boiling tea towels—she was trying so hard. Would it be enough?

"Your mask!" Parker's fingers fumbled at the knotted tea towel at the back of Meredith's neck. She jerked her head away from his touch as she tugged at the clammy cloth.

"Have you no sense?" Parker said, his voice muffled by the handkerchief he was holding in front of his mouth and nose. "It won't do any of us any good if you get sick."

Meredith was certain Parker didn't care whether she got sick; he just didn't want to lose his kitchen slave.

"I'm going up to check on Mr. Harry," Parker said briskly. "In the meantime, I suggest you make yourself presentable. You reek of vinegar."

Once Parker turned his back, she couldn't help sticking out her tongue. It was childish, of course, and if he caught her she'd be in no end of trouble, but at least it helped her feel less like a butterfly pinned to a collector's board, doomed to wait for the rag with the chloroform.

Back in Port Stuart, Meredith had told herself that working in Toronto would be an adventure. So far, it had been nothing but insults, hard work and worry. Well, she knew one person who wouldn't care what she smelled like. She settled into the chair beside the settee and picked up the basin of water. Mrs. Butters moved her head away when the wet cloth touched her skin, but Meredith knew she'd settle in a moment or two.

Meredith shivered, partly from the brisk air flowing in through the open window, partly from the cold water on her hands, and partly from the staggering fatigue that made her head almost too heavy for her neck. She closed her eyes, just long enough to keep the tiredness from dragging her under. It soothed her sore eyes and made her head ache a little less. She could almost believe that the ticking of the kitchen clock was really the mantel clock at home. She'd always thought it had such a lovely chime—

"Why do you have that towel across your face?"

"Oh!" Meredith jerked upright and dropped the towel, her heart pounding. The basin overturned in her lap, the water soaking right through her work apron and the taffeta skirt.

"Are you always that clumsy?" Maggie stood in the doorway in a cream-colored dress with a wide, blue sash, looking fresh and pretty, as if she had dressed for church.

"I asked you a question," Maggie said. "Two questions, actually. You're supposed to answer when someone asks you a question, or don't they teach people that where you come from?"

Meredith tried to calm her hammering heart as she pulled the sodden fabric away from her legs. If she ignored Maggie, maybe Maggie would leave her alone.

"I don't know why Papa ever hired you," Maggie said, her nasty tone at odds with how daintily she was dressed. "I'm going to tell him you've been rude to me."

Mama would say Meredith should be polite, no matter how rude the other person was. It was the first rule of storekeeping. "Is there something I can help you with, Miss Margaret?"

"So you do know how to be polite—when you're worried about your job."

Meredith's wet skirt pulled uncomfortably at her legs as she stood up. She tried not to grimace as she peeled the clinging fabric away from her legs and started toward the kitchen.

Maggie blocked her way. "Why does she sound like that?"

"She has pneumonia." Meredith pulled the towel down from her face as she carried the basin past Maggie and over to the kitchen sink.

"Pneumonia? But my Mama—*people* die from that." Maggie's voice got higher as she dogged Meredith's steps. "How do you know it's pneumonia?"

"Your father said that's what it is."

"What about Harry? Does he have pneumonia, too? Did he catch it from her? Can we catch it from—"

"I don't know!" Meredith hurled the tin basin and its contents into the sink. The satisfying clatter made her wish she could throw Maggie in there, too. She glared out the kitchen window at the leaves of the maple tree in the next yard flaring an angry red. "How do you expect me to know that?"

Purple asters nodded against the wall of the stable.

Meredith fastened her eyes on a black squirrel as it ran along a branch of the maple tree.

"You're not to speak to me like that," Maggie said, after a moment. "And anyway, Harry can't have pneumonia. He just ate too many sandwiches. He'll soon get over a stomach ache. I bet anything he's faking so we'll all feel sorry for him."

Meredith tried to slow her breathing so her voice would be steady. "He's not faking. He's sick and needs tending. Just like Mrs. Butters."

"Well, that's not my job. It's what we have you for, isn't it?" Maggie said, breezily. "I only came down to tell you I want some cocoa. And toast with strawberry jam. You can bring the tray to my room."

"I won't bring it anywhere. Breakfast's over!"

The reckless words were out before Meredith had a chance to bite them back. The *thunk-thunk* of water dripping from the faucet onto the tin basin in the sink sounded loud in her ears as she waited for Maggie's outburst.

"Bring it to my room," Maggie repeated, as if Meredith hadn't said anything at all.

CHAPTER 17

"Hello? Meredith? Is anyone there?"

Tommy! At last! It was nearly noon and Meredith had almost given up on him. She'd taken Maggie some toast and cocoa in the end, and slipped upstairs to change her clothes as Parker had requested, but that had been hours ago. Now she hurried to the back door and beckoned Tommy inside, glad he hadn't forgotten about their outing even though she'd have to disappoint him.

"She looks bad," Tommy said, surprised, when he caught sight of Mrs. Butters. "When did she fall sick?"

"Yesterday. The doctor says it's pneumonia," Meredith hesitated, "and it might even be that Spanish Flu. I'm afraid I can't go out today like we planned."

"Me neither," Tommy said. "That's what I came to tell

you, so I'm glad, in a way, that you can't. Although I wish we could."

"How's your little sister? And your mum?"

"They're still sick, and now Mary's sick, too." Tommy studied the cap in his hands. "I came to ask the doctor what to do. I thought he might help, since Mam works here and everything."

"He's not here. We've been waiting for him all day."

Tommy's face went pale behind his freckles.

"Are they bad?" Meredith asked.

"Mum's the worst, then Mary. Bernie isn't as sick as they are."

"Do you think it's the Spanish Flu?"

"That's what our neighbor thinks. She's awfully afraid of it. She says I should call a doctor or take them to a hospital, but we don't have the money for that. I thought maybe they'd get better if the doctor could tell me what to do. But now I'm afraid—" Tommy turned away from her and looked out the big window over the sink, the muscles in his shoulders working as he crushed his cap.

Meredith reached around him and took hold of his cap to stop him from twisting it into a rag. With his brothers overseas, and his mum and sisters sick, he had nowhere to turn.

"Listen," she said. She recited the instructions Dr. Waterton had given about Mrs. Butters. "And wear a mask," she added, "a towel or something across your nose and mouth, so you don't get it, too."

"All that,"Tommy said, looking so tired that Meredith wondered if he'd been up all night, too, "the sponging and everything, is it helping?"

Meredith wished with all her heart she could say yes, but Tommy deserved the truth. "I'm not sure," she said slowly, "but she isn't getting any worse, and that's a kind of better, isn't it?"

"It's the only kind of better we've got, lassie." Forrest's gruff voice from the back hall startled them. He made his way to the kitchen where he dropped into a chair.

"I'm too old to be up all night. Is there something to eat?" Forrest ran a hand through his hair and rubbed his eyes. "Looks as if you two could do with something yourselves."

Meredith hurried to fill the kettle and set it to boil. "Did the doctor come with you?"

"No, lassie. I'm to check in here and let him know how you're faring. He won't be home until late."

Meredith was certain Mrs. Butters was getting worse, but she'd just have to take care of the cook as best she could until the doctor returned. She removed the cheese from under the china keeper on the kitchen dresser and rummaged in the drawer for a knife. "Is it bad at the hospital?"

"Like the gates of Hell. Sick people arriving every minute, some sounding like poor Elvie there, others delirious with fever." Forrest shook his head. "People shouting and moaning and crying everywhere you turn. The doctor says it's the same at all the hospitals, and there's not much they can do for the poor souls."

"That's dreadful!" Meredith exclaimed. "Those poor, poor people!"

"The doctor says the only way to stop the spread is for people to stay home," Forrest continued, sounding angry. "He says people who go out when they've got sick ones at home should be locked up."

"I…I should get back," Tommy muttered. He turned and fled through the back hall. The screen door banged behind him.

Meredith rounded on Forrest. "That wasn't fair!" she exclaimed. "*You've* been out all day and we've sick people here. He only came here to get help."

Forrest sighed. "I'm sorry, lassie. I'm tired. I didn't mean him. I forgot about his sister."

"It's not just one sister; it's two—*and* his mother." Meredith was tired, too, but no one seemed to think about that. She sawed some cheese off the block of Cheddar, dumped it onto a plate alongside some bread, and banged the plate onto the table in front of Forrest.

"You've a right to be peeved, lassie," Forrest said

ruefully. "I come in here belly-aching, not seeing you've had a long night of it, too."

He reached for a piece of cheese. "Thanks for this. Elvie doesn't sound good. How's young Harry?"

Meredith described the events of the night, careful not to say too much about Parker or Maggie. "I haven't been upstairs for a while," she said. "I've been down here with Mrs. Butters."

"You've had more than enough to do. I'm sure Parker has things well in hand upstairs."

Meredith traced her finger around the wet ring her mug had left on the tabletop.

"Parker does have things well in hand, doesn't he?" Forrest asked, frowning.

She didn't know quite how to answer him. Even though she was sure Forrest would believe her, she didn't want to get into trouble with Parker. "He's been fine."

"I'll bet my last dollar he's been anything but fine—leaving a slip of a girl to manage without a lick of help." Forrest pushed his chair back. "I'm going to pay our friend Parker a visit."

"He's been fine! Really!"

It was too late. Forrest was already heading toward the back stairs. She followed him across the kitchen. "He'll be in Mr. Harry's room!" she called as she climbed the stairs. When she reached the second floor hallway, she saw Forrest leaving the little boy's bedroom and heading for the front staircase. She followed him all the way to the dimly lit third floor, her heart hammering, just in time to see him wrench open the door of the butler's bedroom.

Meredith hovered in the doorway of Parker's sparsely furnished room as Forrest strode over to the bed.

"You shirker!" Forrest roared. "You'd make a bloody useless soldier! It's a good thing King George isn't relying on you. Get your lazy self out of bed!"

Parker's eyes were like giant marbles about to pop out of his head. "You have no right to barge in like this," Parker said, clutching the coverlet to his chin.

Forrest leaned down until they were nearly nose to nose. "I have every right," he said through gritted teeth.

"I will remind you that I am in charge when the doctor is not here," Parker said, squirming out of the way.

Forrest whisked the coverlet off the bed. "Not when you've left that youngster to manage all alone."

Parker quickly pulled the sheet up to cover himself, but not before Meredith caught sight of his bony shoulders and his scrawny neck poking out of his singlet. "I've been up all night, as the girl will tell you."

"As has she," Forrest said, "but she can't take herself off to bed without someone's say so. Now get up."

"I don't take orders from you," Parker said primly.

"I shall most certainly speak to Dr. Waterton about this intrusion."

"And I shall most certainly tell Dr. Waterton that this lassie's been doing the work of two," Forrest said, "while you've been lolling in bed. Now get up! Young Meredith needs sleep more than you do."

Meredith could have hugged him for that. She followed as Forrest stalked out of the room.

He stopped halfway down the hallway and turned to her. "Off to bed, lassie. I'll take care of things."

Nothing had ever felt as good to Meredith as slipping between the cool, smooth sheets in her own little room at the top of the house. Forrest was back, and the doctor would be coming. She wouldn't have to manage on her own any longer.

CHAPTER 18

In the dining room that evening, Meredith nervously eyed the supper she'd assembled: ham sandwiches and a sort of soup she'd created using Mrs. Butters' bottled tomatoes. Parker had protested when she'd asked whether she could serve it in the kitchen, so now it sat looking like a country cousin come to town on the Waterton's elegant china. She was contemplating fetching a jar of pickles from the pantry when Jack appeared.

"Food! I'm starving." He settled into a chair and reached for the platter of sandwiches.

He'd stayed in his room for most of the day, and now Meredith's face grew hot at the memory of his teasing at the party the night before. "I'll call your sister," she said quickly.

"Don't," Jack said, around a mouthful of sandwich. He swallowed. "She'll only gripe and turn up her nose. It'll put me off my Sunday supper." He grinned. "And this is good."

Meredith couldn't help smiling at that. "It's not much of a Sunday supper."

"Who cares? Father's out, Harry's sick, so there's only me and Maggie to please, and she doesn't count."

"I count just as much as you do!" Maggie stood scowling in the doorway. "And don't you forget it."

She'd changed out of her go-to-church clothes into a plain, grey dress. With her hair held back with a band of the same fabric she reminded Meredith of the illustration of a young Quaker girl that she'd seen in a book at school.

"Have some supper, Maggs," Jack said agreeably. "You're always extra grumpy when you're hungry."

"I am not! I'm—" She threw a sour glance at Meredith. "Never mind. I won't argue, not in front of the help."

"The *help* has a name," Jack said. "It wouldn't kill you to learn it." He reached for another sandwich. "Tasty sandwich, *Meredith*."

Maggie lifted a corner of one of the sandwiches. "Ugh! I can't abide ham. And what's that red stuff in the tureen? It looks awful."

"See?" Jack said to Meredith. "I told you she'd gripe

and turn up her nose."

"Jack Waterton! You make me so mad!" Maggie turned to Meredith. "You can go," she said, her nose in the air. "We'll ring if we need you."

Meredith left, fuming. Maggie was just plain rude, and neither of them had asked about Mrs. Butters. In the kitchen, she found Parker sniffing the contents of the soup pot.

"What's this red concoction?" he asked. "It looks awful."

"It's soup," Meredith said. She thought she'd been resourceful in creating a soup out of what she could find, but it seemed her best effort wasn't good enough for anyone at Glenwaring.

"You don't have to eat it if you don't want to," she muttered. She marched to the range, ladled some soup into a waiting bowl and carried it to her place at the table.

She nearly sprayed the first mouthful across the kitchen—they were right, it was awful—but she swallowed it and then grimly refilled her spoon. She knew she shouldn't waste food, but she hesitated before bringing the spoon to her mouth.

Parker inspected the sandwiches she'd kept aside for them, sighed loudly, and then left the kitchen. Meredith hoped he was starving. If he got good and hungry, maybe he wouldn't be so choosy.

She couldn't face finishing the horrible-tasting soup, and it put her off eating anything else, so she covered the plate of sandwiches with a damp tea towel and put it in the icebox in the pantry.

Forrest had promised to be back by eight. Meredith hoped he'd bring the doctor this time, or a nurse—anyone—to help.

She checked on Mrs. Butters, wondering whether she should offer the cook some water, but the prospect of a few blessed minutes of rest persuaded her to wait. The air flowing into the back hall from the open window was brisk, so she shrugged into one of the coats hanging on a hook beside the back door, and then settled into the chair beside the settee.

To pass the time, she decided she'd make a list of all the things she wanted to do in Toronto.

Ride the streetcar.

Explore the shops on Yonge Street.

Visit Mr. Eaton's store.

Buy some shoes—that should have been first—smart black ones, with a little heel and a design stamped into the leather.

Find the nearest library. Papa had told her people could borrow as many books as they liked from the free public lending libraries in Toronto. She longed for a book she could keep in her apron pocket for moments of quiet like this. Even if she couldn't finish school right now, she could keep up her education by reading so she wouldn't be so far behind when she did go back.

Of course, Parker wouldn't like it if he caught her reading while she was supposed to be working, but she could always read at night in bed in her little room upstairs. He couldn't stop her doing that, although he still seemed bent on finding fault with everything she did. Mama would say that the good in people always evened out the bad in the end, but Mama wouldn't say that if she met Parker.

Thinking about Mama started another round of worries: Would the Spanish Flu reach Port Stuart? What if Mama got sick? Or Ellen?

The kitchen clock began its whirring and clanging to announce the hour. As if on cue, she heard an automobile pull up and soon, Forrest was hanging his coat on a hook beside the back door. She was disappointed to see that the doctor wasn't with him, but then she realized that the doctor would use the front door. He might just this minute be coming up the walk.

"It's cold for October," Forrest said. He hung his cap on the hook with his coat and smoothed his hair. "Is there any supper, lassie? There's little to eat at the hospital, and I've been carting mattresses from floor to floor all day long. How are young Harry, and Elvie here?"

"Parker says Harry's about the same, but Mrs. Butters is really sick," Meredith slipped the borrowed coat off and hung it on the back of her chair before following him into the kitchen. "Did Dr. Waterton come with you?"

"No, lassie." Forrest pulled a chair out from the table and sat down heavily. "Can you fetch the others? He's asked me to talk to all of you."

"You mean Parker?"

"Jack and Maggie, too."

Meredith brought him the plate of sandwiches from the icebox along with a jar of pickles. "It's serious, then?"

"Aye, lassie. I'll tell you all about it once everyone's here."

Meredith climbed the stairs to thc sccond floor, and then knocked at Maggie's door.

"Yes?"

Meredith pushed the door open. Maggie was lying on her bed in a nest of lacy pillows, a pink-and-white coverlet bunched around her. In the light of the bedside lamp, the room glowed softly pink like the inside of Mama's prized conch shell on the mantel back home. A tray holding a mug and an empty plate sat on the dresser. Maggie seemed intent on the book she was holding.

"Excuse me, Miss Margaret. Forrest asked me to fetch you."

"So?" One blonde eyebrow went up.

"He says we're to have a meeting."

"That has nothing to do with me." Maggie lazily turned a page, her eyes fixed on her book. "Besides, I'm not a ball or a bucket. I can't be *fetched* at someone's say so."

Meredith didn't know why Maggie was always so rude when her father was so kind. Well, she'd said what she'd come to say. Whether Maggie came downstairs or not wasn't her concern.

Maggie flicked her eyes toward Meredith. "Take the tray when you go."

"Aren't you the grand lady?" Jack's mocking voice came from behind Meredith's shoulder. He strode over to the bed and plucked the book from Maggie's hands. "You could at least be polite."

"Don't you have anything better to do than stand in the hallway eavesdropping?" Maggie lifted her chin.

"Nope." He leaned down until his face was inches from Maggie's. "Get yourself downstairs like she said."

"Why should I?"

"Because Father's not here. Because I'm in charge." Jack glowered at his sister, "Because it's *my* say so."

Maggie narrowed her eyes. "For your information, John Temple Waterton, you're not in charge of me."

Nevertheless, Meredith thought something Jack had said must have registered because Maggie sat up and swung her legs over the side of the bed.

"I don't need you or Forrest or that girl telling me what to do," Maggie said. "I'll come downstairs, but she can take the tray. It's her job, after all." She swept past Meredith and out the door.

The sudden silence in the room seemed even louder to Meredith than their argument. "Thanks," she said to Jack. "She wouldn't listen to me."

"She doesn't listen to anyone," Jack said. "Mama would never have let her get away with being rude like that. I figured it was my job to keep her in line."

"It was nice of you all the same," Meredith said as she picked up the tray.

"Leave it," Jack said. "Let her take it."

"It's my job, Mr. Jack, like she said." Meredith knew that if Maggie complained, Parker would make her life miserable. She carried the tray into the hall.

"Do you know what this is about?" Jack asked as he followed her to the back stairs.

"Some of it," Meredith said. "Forrest will explain it all."

"It must be serious," Jack said.

CHAPTER 19

Maggie slouched, arms crossed, in the chair beside Jack on one side of the long kitchen table. Meredith and Forrest sat facing them on the other side. Meredith thought they looked like the pictures of the peace talks in the newspaper, although the sullen look on Maggie's face said this wasn't likely to be peaceful. They were waiting for Parker.

They could hear Mrs. Butters' ragged wheezing from the back hall. Jack had said they should sit in the dining room, but, to Meredith's relief, Forrest had insisted they be close to Mrs. Butters. Meredith worried about Harry waking up alone upstairs, but Parker had made it clear all along that he would take care of Harry so she supposed she should let him do the worrying, too.

Parker strode into the room at last and took his usual seat at the head of the table, with Meredith on his right. An acrid smell of camphor made Meredith's eyes water. She'd smelled traces of it in the third floor hallway earlier, and now it seemed to be coming from Parker himself. She edged her chair away as discreetly as she could, careful to breathe through her mouth, but the searing odor was relentless. Jack's and Maggie's scrunched-up faces told her she wasn't the only one suffering.

Parker cleared his throat. "Before Forrest begins—"

"Before I begin," Forrest said, "what in blazes is that smell, Parker?"

"It smells like moths," Maggie said.

"Camphor, Miss Margaret," Parker said, reddening, "not moths. Mrs. Butters uses it to safeguard the woolen blankets against moths over the summer months."

"But it's October," Jack said. "Why do we smell it now?"

"It's a preventive, Mr. Jack," Parker said primly. "You'd be well advised to do the same."

"Do what, exactly?" asked Maggie. "And why, if it's going to stink like that?"

"A small bag of camphor worn next to the skin is said to ward off the germs," Parker explained.

Meredith thought Maggie was about to ask Parker another question, but Jack jumped in.

"Forrest, can you please tell us what's going on?" he asked. "We know Harry's sick, and all Parker would tell me earlier was that Mrs. Butters might have pneumonia, and that Maggie and I should stay away from them both. But there's more to it than that, isn't there?"

"Aye, laddie," Forrest said. "You've heard of that Spanish Flu that's in the papers?"

Jack nodded. "They were talking about it at dinner last night."

"Aye. And you've maybe heard how the soldiers are falling ill overseas," Forrest continued, "and people have come down with it in Boston and Montreal?"

People weren't just coming down with it. Meredith had read that hundreds of them were dying. She shuddered.

"But what's that to do with us?" Maggie's question caught Meredith by surprise. Did they really not know?

"It's been confirmed here in Toronto, and it's worse than anyone predicted." Forrest briefly filled them in on the situation at the hospital.

"It looks like Toronto is in for a rough time of it," he concluded. "Your father needs to stay at the hospital for the time being to help manage the crisis, and he thinks Mrs. Butters and young Mr. Harry will get better care here."

"Are you saying Mrs. Butters and Harry have the Spanish Flu?" Jack asked.

Forrest looked at him for a long moment. "Mrs. Butters almost certainly. So far it seems to affect healthy adults most severely. The doctor's not sure about Mr. Harry."

"What arrangements have been made about a nurse?" Parker asked.

Forrest shook his head. "None to be had, I'm afraid."

"None?" Parker scowled. "That's ridiculous. Surely Dr. Waterton, the Chief of Medicine at Toronto City Hospital, can arrange for—"

Forrest held up his hand. "All of the hospitals are short-handed. The nurses they do have are working round the clock preparing for the onslaught, and Dr. Waterton feels they should stay where they're most needed. He's even asked me to return to the hospital after this to help transport patients."

No doctor, no nurse, no Forrest—no one—to help. The seedling of hope Meredith had been carefully tending since Forrest arrived withered to nothing.

"But he's coming home soon, right?" Jack's face was eager.

"He'll come as soon as he can, lad."

Maggie sat up at that. "What's that mean? When will he be coming home?"

Forrest sighed. "The hospital's reeling, Miss Maggie. He can't leave just yet, not while the doctors and nurses are stretched to the limit. They're even calling in retired doctors and nurses to help out. It's not what he wants, you understand, but Parker will be here, after all."

The corners of Parker's mouth tweaked into a small smile. Meredith was afraid that meant he'd be even more difficult now.

"Did he say what we're to do?" Jack asked.

Forrest nodded. "First of all, and he stressed this: no one's to go out."

"But I'll miss Abby's party!" Maggie exclaimed.

"Stay home from school?" Jack protested. "Father's always at me about my grades!"

"He means the children, of course, and I fully agree," Parker said. "They will need to be kept home in case they catch something."

"Not just the children," Forrest said.

"You can't be serious!" Parker scowled. "None of us?"

Forrest nodded glumly.

"I know there's been talk of quarantine," Parker began, "but surely if we're careful—"

"Doctor's orders," Forrest said, with finality. "All of you are to stay here to keep from spreading it. No school, no visits to friends, nothing. And no visitors."

It felt to Meredith as if the ceiling was pressing down on them, the walls squeezing closer. The Spanish Flu had only just arrived in Toronto, but she'd read that cities such as Boston had been battling it for weeks. Weeks of being cooped up together—with Parker, with Maggie—stretched bleakly in front of her.

"Then why are you here?" Maggie asked. "You've been at the hospital. You could be spreading it to others now that you're out. Why is it all right for you to go out and not us?"

Much as Meredith hated to admit it, Maggie Waterton was clever.

"It's not all right, Miss Maggie. The doctor told me to stay well away from anyone outside of Glenwaring," Forrest said. He sighed. "You've already been exposed, you see," he added gently.

The look of horror on Maggie's face showed she'd only just now understood the risks they faced right here at home. "So you're saying we'll get it, too?"

"Not necessarily," Forrest said. "Your father sent some masks to guard against infection—" He rummaged in his pocket and pulled out a handful of bunched cloth. "These are what the nurses wear. Parker can explain about them." He picked a rectangle out of the bunch and held it up, strings dangling.

"Is there anything else?" Jack asked.

"Give them water when they can take it, then soft foods: soup, an egg, custard. Meredith knows about that."

"I don't like custard." Harry stood unsteadily at the bottom of the back stairs. Meredith thought that he must be feeling better to have come downstairs on his own. Maybe Mrs. Butters would turn a corner soon, too.

"Mr. Harry!" Parker said sternly. "I gave you express instructions to stay in bed while I was gone."

"I don't want to stay in bed." Harry sat down on the bottom step as if his legs couldn't hold him up anymore. "I want Jack to play a game with me."

Parker sighed. "Mr. Jack is busy just now. Meredith will take you back upstairs."

"No-o-o!" Harry wailed. "I don't want her. I want Jack!"

"Hang on, Parker," Jack said, to Meredith's surprise. "Harry, come and sit with me. We'll soon be done."

Parker frowned. "Mr. Jack, the doctor's orders were—"

"It's all right, Parker," Jack replied. "It's got to be lonely up there all by himself."

And not much better with only Parker for company, Meredith thought.

"Then put on a mask and go sit over there with him," Forrest said, pushing a mask across the table to Jack, who made a face. "You must take it seriously, Mr. Jack. You, too, Miss Maggie. There's too much at stake."

Jack tied the mask over his nose and mouth as he headed toward the staircase. "I feel silly."

"You look it," Maggie said. "I'm not wearing any stupid mask."

Jack joined Harry on the step and hoisted the little boy into his lap. Harry put his thumb in his mouth, rested his head on Jack's chest and blinked out at them.

The need to check on Mrs. Butters set Meredith's fingers to worrying the edge of her apron. They'd been sitting here much too long.

"I'll continue, shall I?" Forrest looked around the table. "Pneumonia can develop very quickly—we've all seen poor Mrs. Butters—but Dr. Waterton says good nursing makes a difference. And maybe young Mr. Harry here is an example of that."

"He only had a stomach ache, if you ask me," Maggie muttered.

"No one did ask you," Jack said sharply, his voice muffled by his mask. "Keep your opinions to yourself."

Meredith was certain Maggie would flounce out of the room at that, but she only twirled one of her curls around her finger as idly as if they were talking about a church picnic instead of a terrifying illness.

"Forrest, how long…how long until—" Jack stopped.

Meredith was sure he meant to ask "until they get better," but "until they die" was echoing in her head. The newspapers reported that some people had died within a day of coming down with the Spanish Flu. Could Mrs. Butters die just as quickly as she'd become sick?

"No telling, lad. It's a demon sickness. You're to keep

a close watch." Forrest cleared his throat. "Mr. Jack, the doctor asked me to tell you he's counting on you to keep things working here."

Jack sat up a little straighter. Maggie rolled her eyes.

"That's as it should be, I suppose." Parker said, looking as if he'd swallowed something disagreeable.

"So someone needs to stay with Mrs. Butters," Jack said, "and someone with Harry, at least until Father comes. Is that right?"

"I've already seen to that, Mr. Jack," Parker said quickly. "Meredith will continue to watch over Mrs. Butters, and I myself will ensure that Mr. Harry has the best of care. There's no need for you or Miss Margaret to concern yourselves."

Stung into speaking, Meredith began, "But there's more than just watching—"

"I've already seen to it, as I said," Parker stated in a tone and with a look that said Meredith wasn't to argue.

"Hang on a moment," Forrest said. "Meredith's got a point. If no one's going out, there's also no one coming in. That means no cook or daily, and everyone's got to eat, after all, and someone's got to clean up."

Meredith could have hugged him, but the four sets of eyes that focused on her made her squirm instead.

"As you well know, Forrest, Meredith is under my direction, as are *all* the staff at Glenwaring," Parker replied.

"I want to assure Mr. Jack and Miss Margaret that we will do whatever needs to be done."

His oily smile in their direction only confirmed Meredith's suspicion about who'd be doing whatever needed to be done. She glanced sidelong at Forrest, who looked troubled, but he remained quiet.

"All right then," Jack said, "I think we have a plan."

"It's not much of a plan: We're to stay locked into the same house with someone who's so sick she might die?" Maggie's eyes flashed a challenge at her brother. "I have a better one: Forrest should take Mrs. Butters to the hospital."

"But that's not what Father wants," Jack said, glaring at his sister. "He said they'd get better care here. He's left me in charge, and I say we follow his orders."

Jack and Maggie seemed to be embarking on some kind of war and Meredith didn't know where to look. She felt as if she was slowly stewing in the steam from the copper boiler where the tea towels she and Parker had used as masks were churning in the simmering water.

"Since you're in charge, Jack," Maggie said at last, her words barbed, "maybe you can answer this: Just what's your plan going to be when the rest of us get sick?"

CHAPTER 20

Forrest had returned to the hospital after the meeting, taking a change of clothes for the doctor, but only after he'd had a long conversation with Parker.

"Mind he helps out," was all Forrest had said to Meredith before he left. Nevertheless, Parker had surprised her when he offered to sit with Mrs. Butters for part of the night so she could rest. Clearly, Forrest's words had made an impression. She wondered how long it would last.

Meredith woke the next morning to find that the Spanish Flu had stormed into Toronto. Under the heading "Yesterday's Dead," the newspaper reported the names of twenty-five people who had died the previous day, and the toll was expected to rise as more people became infected. The hospitals were struggling to meet the need for emergency care. Citizens were warned to stay off the streetcars for fear of catching or spreading the germs in crowded spaces. The closure of schools, churches and places where people gathered was being debated.

Postmen were given cards to distribute along their routes for people to fill out and leave at the door if they needed help. Church groups, clubs and associations were advertising for volunteers to nurse the sick or prepare food in hastily set-up soup kitchens. Anxious workers faced difficult choices: stay home and lose a day's wages, or go out and risk contracting the Spanish Flu. Either way, families were in jeopardy.

But it was Parker's worrying about his health that unnerved Meredith. He no longer derided newspaper coverage of the Spanish Flu as "hysterical nonsense." Instead, he searched the newspaper for preventives. He sprinkled hot coals with brown sugar and sulfur, and then inhaled the choking smoke while Meredith fled with her apron over her nose. He tied a handkerchief overtop of the gauze mask from the hospital "for extra protection against airborne germs." The bulky combination made him sound as if he were speaking from behind a pillow. He even asked Meredith whether Mrs. Butters kept a store of goose grease so he could make a poultice for his chest. He seemed to put his faith in every so-called cure-all, even though the medical authorities said such measures were unlikely to help.

Maggie pointedly kept as far away as she could from Harry and Mrs. Butters, but Jack played games with Harry to keep him quiet. He seemed to take the responsibility of being in charge seriously. He wasn't turning out to be as self-centered as Meredith had thought.

Parker had taken Jack's offer to play with Harry as an opportunity to announce that he had one of his headaches and needed to spend some time in a darkened room. Meredith resented that, even though she knew he was entitled to a rest after sitting up with Mrs. Butters during the night. However, there was nothing she could do about it, so she decided she'd browse the cook's dog-eared copy of *Mrs. Beeton's Book of Household Management* while she sat with Mrs. Butters.

She settled into the chair by the settee and opened the book to the chapter on soup.

"*The principal art in composing good rich soup,*" she read, "*is to so proportion the several ingredients that the flavor of one shall not predominate over another, and that all the articles of which it is composed shall form an agreeable whole.*"

Meredith was pondering why her soup definitely had not formed "an agreeable whole" when the doorbell sounded. Parker generally answered the front door, but he was unlikely to hear it upstairs. Mrs. Butters seemed settled, so Meredith headed for the front door as the doorbell sounded again. She smoothed her hair, straightened her apron and tugged her sleeves down. She debated leaving her mask in place, but took it off instead and stuffed it in the pocket of her apron.

When she opened the door, she found Mrs. Stinson standing on the verandah in a trim navy coat, a glossy, black bird wing front and center on her stylish hat.

"Don't stand there gawping, girl. I can see you are not used to greeting visitors." Mrs. Stinson swept past Meredith and into the front hall.

The doctor had said no visitors. "I'm sorry, Mrs. Stinson, you can't—"

"Where is the butler?" Mrs. Stinson's sharp eyes darted around the hallway.

"Parker's not available right now, ma'am, but—"

"No matter. The cook will be expecting me." She ran a gloved finger along the mantel of the hall fireplace, and then frowned as she examined it. "My clients know I am diligent in ensuring that the new help meets expectations."

She means me, Meredith thought resentfully. She'll be calling me "Margaret" any minute. "Mrs. Butters is sick," she said carefully.

Mrs. Stinson paused in her tour of inspection. "Sick? Well-bred people don't say 'sick,' Margaret, they say 'indisposed.'"

"I'm sorry, ma'am. Mrs. Butters is indisposed."

"That's better. I hope it is nothing serious?"

Meredith hesitated, but only for a moment. "Dr. Waterton thinks she has the Spanish Influenza."

"Oh, my goodness!" Mrs. Stinson's hand flew to her mouth. "I didn't think...How could...? And in *Rosedale*..." Mrs. Stinson backed away. "And *you* might be...in Rosedale!"

She yanked the front door open, and nearly leapt onto the verandah. "I'll call some other time," she said quickly, then scuttled down the steps and along the path to the waiting cab like a beetle scurrying for cover.

"Crabby old cow!"

Meredith looked up to see Jack grinning down at her from the top of the stairs.

"You gave her a scare," Jack said.

"I did, didn't I?" Meredith couldn't help a grin of her own as Jack took the steps two at a time and joined her in the open doorway. Mama would say it wasn't right to upset people, but how could Mrs. Stinson believe that people in Rosedale would escape the Spanish Flu? Did she really think money and mansions would keep people safe?

They watched a pair of black horses round the corner, harnesses jingling, tall black plumes waving from silver head plates. The driver was sitting up tall on the bench of the wagon in his black suit and top hat. A small, white coffin topped with a spray of creamy lilies lay in the back of the wagon. A second pair and wagon followed the first, this one carrying a longer gray coffin, also draped in lilies. A single automobile completed the procession.

A double funeral, thought Meredith, shivering, the white casket for a child, the gray one for a mother, maybe, or a father. People all over the city were dying from the Spanish Flu.

Meredith knew about death and funerals—Papa, of course, and Granddad—but the portrait of Mrs. Waterton looking down at them from across the hall reminded her that Jack and his family did, too.

They drew back into the house as Meredith closed the heavy door. She prayed that the click of the latch would keep them safe.

CHAPTER 21

Somehow they made it through the night. Parker mostly kept his distance by tending to Harry upstairs, leaving Meredith to worry over Mrs. Butters' increasingly wheezy breathing. He telephoned the hospital periodically to try and contact Dr. Waterton, but the nurses scolded him that the lines needed to be kept free for more urgent calls.

"As if I'm wasting their time," Parker had complained to Meredith that morning. "As if I didn't have the sense to know what is, and is not, appropriate."

That had been hours ago, and she hadn't seen him since. Now she was unpacking a box of groceries at the kitchen table. The store had sent everything she'd asked Parker to order: eggs, onions, bread, tea, carrots, beans, ham, apples, and a small packet of sugar.

"Where's Parker?"

Meredith looked up to see Jack framed in the kitchen doorway. She was glad to have some company at last. "Upstairs, I think."

"Harry's throwing soldiers around his room," Maggie announced, pushing past Jack into the kitchen. Meredith definitely wasn't happy to see her.

"Blast that Harry!" Jack frowned. "He's more work now that he's feeling better. You could at least take a turn sitting with him, Maggie."

"He doesn't want me," Maggie replied airily. She reached for one of the apples Meredith had set in a blue bowl on the kitchen table. "He wants to play some game with you."

"I'm looking for Parker," Jack said.

"Sure you are, here in the kitchen with Marjorie, or whatever her name is." Maggie waved her hand in Meredith's direction. "If you're really looking for him, send her up to see if he's in his room."

Maggie talked as if Meredith was a chair or a table, something to be used when needed, not a person with feelings and a mind of her own.

"I should send you up instead," Jack said to his sister, "seeing as *Meredith's* busy."

Maggie ignored him and leveled her gaze at Meredith. "Don't think he likes you," she said, each word honed to a point. "Jack flirts with all the kitchen girls. It's pathetic how they all fall for it."

They all fall for it.

Had Jack been flirting with her? Maybe at first—when he'd stood so close the night before the party, when he'd made a game of tugging at her skirt—but Meredith was certain he'd been different lately. He talked to her and seemed to really listen to her replies, as if she had something to say. But now she wondered whether it was just a game he was playing.

Maggie started for the back stairs. "I'll see if I can find Parker for you, Jack," she said, sweetly, but there were barbs on those words, too. "I'd hate for you to cut short your cozy time with Marilla there."

Meredith squirmed. Maggie had done it again, twisted a perfectly ordinary conversation between her and Jack into something small and mean.

Meredith startled when Jack touched her arm.

"Don't listen to her," he said. "Maggie's a troublemaker."

He certainly looked sincere, but Meredith didn't know what to believe. Was he flirting? How would she tell?

"I'd better go up to Harry," Jack was saying, "before he causes real damage. He could singlehandedly put an end to the war by launching those lead soldiers of his at the Huns! I wish he'd let Maggie sit with him, but—"

A scream from upstairs stopped Jack's words, and then sent him pounding up the back stairs. Meredith raced after him all the way to the third floor where Maggie stood shrieking in the hallway outside Parker's room, her hands over her eyes.

"Stop, Maggie!" Jack pried her hands from her face. "What is it?"

Maggie snatched her hands from his grasp and twisted away, sobbing. Meredith took a deep breath and moved to the doorway of Parker's room.

Parker was slumped over the writing desk by the window, his head on the desk top, his face turned toward the door. His eyes were closed. Something dark had spilled across the top of the desk. At first, Meredith thought he'd knocked over his inkwell.

Then she realized it wasn't ink.

She'd never seen so much blood: a lake spreading outward from Parker's cheek, a thin stream spilling over the edge of the desk onto the floor, spattering Parker's shoes. She leaned against the door frame to stop her head from spinning.

"Can you see where's it coming from?" Jack stood beside her now. Maggie was whimpering from somewhere behind them.

"I'm not sure," Meredith said, her stomach churning. "His nose?"

Jack stepped past her and grabbed a towel from the washstand in the corner. He pressed the towel against Parker's nose. Blood from the table top seeped into the rough fabric.

"Do you think it's the Spanish Flu?" Jack asked, pulling his mask into place with his other hand.

"Maybe." Meredith said, tugging hers up, too, and trying to remember what she'd read in the newspaper.

Jack gingerly lifted the towel away from Parker's face. A thin red stream trickled from one nostril. "You're right, it's his nose. Looks like it's stopping." His words were muffled by his mask. "I suppose we should move him."

He shook the butler's shoulder. "Parker! Can you sit up?"

Parker moaned.

"Steady his head," Jack said to Meredith, handing her the towel.

Meredith held it to Parker's nose and slid her other hand under Parker's bald head, her fingers recoiling from the blood on the table top. She wanted to scream, but she bit down hard instead. She told herself it was no worse than cutting up meat for stew: there was always blood on the cutting board. "Ready," she said, through clenched teeth.

Jack positioned himself behind the chair and slipped his hands under Parker's shoulders. "Let's get him to the bed."

Parker spluttered as Jack hauled him out of the chair. Blood peppered Parker's shirt front and dripped onto her sleeve as Meredith struggled to keep hold of his blood-slicked head. Between them, they shuffled him over to the narrow bed against the wall, Parker stumbling between them.

Parker coughed as they lowered him to the mattress, and Meredith squealed as a dark gob of congealed blood splatted onto her apron. Gurgling noises came from his throat.

"He's choking!" Meredith cried. "Sit him up!"

They heaved him to a sitting position. Parker's eyes opened briefly, widened, then fluttered closed.

"He's bleeding again." Jack wedged the thin pillow behind Parker's back, while Meredith pressed the towel to his nose, trying to keep her fingers from touching his skin. She thought she might throw up if her fingers got bloody again.

"You wouldn't think he'd have any left," Jack muttered.

"Is Parker sick?" Harry stood in the doorway, wrapped in a blue blanket. Maggie stood behind him, her eyes fastened on Parker. She'd stopped crying.

"He shouldn't see this," Meredith whispered to Jack. "It'll give him nightmares."

"You were told to stay in bed, Harry." Jack crossed the room and knelt in front of his brother.

"I heard noises and I didn't know where you were." Harry fingered the satin edging of his blanket. "Is Parker sick?"

"Yes," Jack said. "Now go back to your room. I'll come in a minute."

"I can't. My legs are wobbly again," Harry said. He sank to the floor and leaned against the door frame. The blue veins at his temples showed through his pale skin.

"Take Harry downstairs, Maggie," Jack said.

Maggie shook her head.

"I don't want her," Harry said.

Jack looked at his sister for a long moment. "Fine. Don't even try to help." He held his arms out to his brother. "Come on, Harry." He bundled the little boy and his blanket into his arms, but Maggie blocked his way.

"You realize we'll have to watch Parker now, too!" she cried, her words echoing in the hallway.

Harry, Mrs. Butters, now Parker. The look on Jack's face reflected what Meredith was thinking: How would they manage? And who'd be next?

CHAPTER 22

Meredith lugged the nearly full coal scuttle through the back hall that evening, thinking that the prospect of mice or worse in the cellar was the least of her worries. At least, keeping busy prevented her thoughts from endlessly circling the memory of Parker's face lying in a pool of blood. She'd scrubbed her hands for a long time afterward to remove all traces of that blood.

Jack had been telephoning the hospital, but on the rare occasions when he managed to get through, he'd been scolded for tying up the line. He achieved one small victory, however, when he at last persuaded Maggie to sit with Harry. Harry didn't really need anyone watching him while he slept, but Maggie made a fuss about how much she was helping.

Meredith was convinced Maggie had chosen to sit with Harry to avoid the unpleasantness of caring for Mrs. Butters or Parker. It was fine for Maggie to play the fine lady, but some people weren't given a choice about what they did.

Jack had insisted on cleaning up the mess in Parker's room. Meredith had been impressed by how he'd scrubbed the desk and the floor to remove all traces of blood. However, Parker's ruined clothing defeated Meredith. She finally rolled his blood-stained shirt and singlet into a ball along with her spattered apron and Jack's shirt and stashed them in the laundry hamper. Mrs. O'Hagan could tackle them when life returned to normal.

Mrs. Butters had been sleeping restlessly on the settee, the blanket Meredith had tucked around her rising and falling with every rasping breath. Jack had assured Meredith he'd keep an eye on Parker, so Meredith was free to doze in the chair beside Mrs. Butters all afternoon, too afraid to leave the cook's side in case the awful choking started again.

But dozing in the chair wasn't proper sleeping, and now Meredith's brain felt like cotton wool. She was shoveling the night's load of coal into the firebox of the range when Maggie and Jack burst into the kitchen.

"Send her!" Maggie shouted, pointing to Meredith.

"No!" Jack roared.

"I don't care what you say or do," Maggie shot back.

"I'm not going up there! I've got my hands full with Harry."

"We've all got our hands full," Jack said. "That's no excuse."

"I'll tell you what's *no excuse:* there's *no excuse* for not taking them to the hospital!" Maggie's eyes were blazing.

"Father said we're to stay, so we're staying." Jack crossed his arms and drew himself up so that he towered over his sister. "And until he tells me something different, I don't want to hear any more about it!"

"Jack, listen to me!" Maggie took a deep breath. "Papa doesn't know Parker's sick, he thinks Parker is helping manage things here. How do you know what he'd tell us to do now? Ask her," Maggie said, pointing her chin at Meredith. "I bet she agrees with me."

Jack glared at his sister, and then stormed out of the kitchen, ignoring Meredith completely. She'd thought she and Jack were allies of a sort, working together, doing what had to be done. It had been the only good thing that had come out of this awful day, and now even that had fizzled. Jack clearly hadn't seen it the way she did.

"He makes me so mad I could punch him!" Maggie exclaimed, dropping into a chair at the table. "But I suppose you think he's right?"

Meredith scooped the last few coals into the range while she sorted out her thoughts. "I don't know who's right," she said at last.

She hung the scoop on the iron rack at the side of the

stove and brushed traces of coal dust from her skirt. "He's only doing what your father told him to do. It's hard to know what the right thing is now that Parker's sick."

"Jack's being stupid," Maggie grumbled, but she looked drained of the anger that had fuelled her a moment ago. She chose a red apple from the bowl on the table and rubbed it against her skirt. "And he's even more stupid if he can't see that." She bit into the apple, sending a spurt of juice dribbling down her chin.

A sudden choking sound erupted in the back hall. Meredith tugged her mask up as she rushed to Mrs. Butters' side. She tried to lean the cook forward while at the same time pounding her on the back to help clear her lungs. Mrs. Butters gagged and choked and sputtered.

Maggie hovered uncertainly in the doorway from the kitchen, her hand over her mouth. She flinched and turned her face away when Mrs. Butters began spewing wads of greenish-yellow phlegm onto the blanket that covered her. When the spasm eased, Mrs. Butters' face was deep purple and wet with sweat.

Meredith helped Mrs. Butters lie back against the pillows propped on the settee. She fished a cloth out of the basin of water on the floor and wiped Mrs. Butters' face, then used it to gather up the mess on the blanket.

"Is it always that bad?" Maggie's voice was shaky as she followed Meredith into the kitchen.

Meredith was too angry to answer. Mrs. Butters could have died right there and Maggie would have stood by and watched like some helpless princess.

"Do you think she'll get better?" Maggie asked.

Meredith tossed the wadded-up cloth and its contents into the firebox of the range where it hissed and sent up clouds of steam. Meredith watched through the firebox opening until the edge of the cloth blackened and a small yellow flame licked along the edge.

"I don't know," she replied, closing the firebox door. There was no point in being angry at Maggie. It certainly wouldn't change anything. "I hope so."

"I know Parker's not as sick as Mrs. Butters," Maggie said, "but what happens if he gets like that—or worse?"

Meredith looked up and studied the other girl's anxious face. "We'll just do the best we can," she said, "and then pray that it's enough."

✚✚✚

Later that evening, Meredith read the newspaper with mounting horror: half the nursing staff of the Grace Hospital had come down with the Spanish Flu. The Toronto Western Hospital and St. Michaels' Hospital were full and had stopped accepting patients. City workers had removed the carpets, sterilized the beds, and disinfected the mattresses in two former hotels to turn them into makeshift hospitals. The newspaper said readers shouldn't worry if they were taking precautions, but Parker had been taking precautions, and he'd sickened in spite of them.

"Can you come upstairs?"

Meredith looked up from the paper to see Harry Waterton standing at the bottom of the back stairs, shifting from one foot to the other. She glanced at the kitchen clock.

"It's after eight," she said, crossing the kitchen to stand beside him. "What are you doing out of bed?"

"Jack said I had to get you."

"What was Mr. Jack doing in your room?" Where was Maggie? Jack should have been upstairs with Parker.

"I wanted him to play a game with me, but—" Harry leaned closer, "he threw up. And then he told me to get you."

"Oh, no!" Meredith grabbed Harry's hand and started up the stairs. She told herself it couldn't be the Spanish Flu: Jack was probably overtired, they all were, or maybe the ham had gone off.

But when she reached Harry's room, she found Jack sprawled in the rocking chair beside Harry's bed. His mask was bunched around his neck, streaked with vomit.

Harry held his nose. "It stinks in here."

Meredith tugged her mask up as Jack's eyes turned to her.

"Sorry," he whispered, but Meredith wasn't in the mood for apologies. Now he'd have to be sponged and watched like the others.

And where was Maggie? Not here with her sick brother, and not up with Parker either, Meredith was certain. She stalked out of the room and down the hall to Maggie's bedroom, Harry at her heels. She knocked on the closed door but didn't wait for an answer before pushing it open.

Maggie Waterton was sitting at the dressing table, holding a set of long, sparkly earrings on either side of her face, admiring herself in the mirror. She startled at the intrusion and got quickly to her feet. "You can't just barge in here like that!" she exclaimed.

For a moment, Meredith was too angry to speak. "Your brother's sick!" Meredith declared. "I need your help."

"What are you talking about? Harry's fine," Maggie said. "See for yourself. He's standing behind you."

"No, not him. It's—"

"Jack? He can't be."

When Meredith didn't answer, the earrings dropped from Maggie's hand. Then Maggie rushed past her and ran down the hall.

CHAPTER 23

"We'll have to take him to the hospital," Maggie announced a few moments later, scowling at Meredith as if Jack being sick was something Meredith had cooked up to annoy her.

"No," Jack mumbled. "Father...better here."

Maggie turned on him, her hands on her hips. "You don't get a say. I'm in charge now."

"Then can we take Mrs. Butters, too?" Meredith asked eagerly. "She's much sicker than—" she paused, realizing Maggie might not see the situation the way she did. "She's just so sick," she amended, hoping the memory of Mrs. Butters struggling to breathe would change Maggie's mind.

"Oh, all right," Maggie said to Meredith's relief.

"Parker, too, I suppose. But we'll take Jack first. I'm going to telephone the hospital and tell them to send Forrest immediately. And I'm going to keep on phoning until they send him."

She turned toward the door, but Harry blocked her way. "Move, Harry."

"Is Papa coming home?" Harry looked up at his sister.

"I'm going to telephone him now." Maggie tried hustling him aside, but he was determined to stay put.

"Can I talk to him?"

"No, you can't! This is serious, Harry." Maggie sidled past him into the hallway.

Harry's face crumpled. "I hate you!" he wailed. "I want Papa!"

Meredith bent down and tried to take Harry's hands, but he snatched them out of her grasp. He stiffened when she put her arm around him, but after a moment he let himself relax into her side.

"Hush now, Mr. Harry," Meredith said. "It's serious, just as she said, but you're a brave boy, and I'm going to tell your father that when he comes home."

Harry drew away from her and looked into her eyes. "Really?"

"Really, truly," Meredith said. "But right now I need your help."

"I'm a good helper!"

"I know you are. I need you to stay with your brother while your sister and I work out what to do. Can you do that?"

Harry nodded.

"Good boy. Come and find me if he gets sick again or starts coughing." She gave him a hug and then sped along the hall toward the front stairs.

"Miss Margaret," she called over the railing. She could see Maggie sitting in the telephone alcove near the front door. "Wait!"

"You're right about taking them to the hospital," Meredith said, panting, when she reached the alcove. Maggie was searching through the pages of the small, leather-bound book that sat on the shelf beside the telephone. "But what if you can't get through to someone who will listen? The nurses wouldn't help Parker or your brother."

Maggie frowned. "Then I'll telephone for a cab," she said. "That's what Mama used to do when Forrest was out."

"A cab mightn't come," Meredith stepped gingerly through the minefield of Maggie's words, "not if you tell them it's to take someone to the hospital. And even if you don't tell them, as soon as the driver sees your brother, he'll know."

"I hadn't thought of that." Maggie sighed. "Then I'll tell the hospital it's an emergency—it *is* one now—and that I must speak to my father right away." She looked down at the little book. "Here it is: Toronto City Hospital."

The Waterton's telephone looked like a tall black candlestick with a bell-shaped earpiece hanging from a hook on the side. In Port Stuart, Meredith had only ever seen the wooden box type that hung on the wall. She wondered how you alerted the operator on this one, since there was no crank.

Maggie steadied the base of the telephone with one hand. She lifted the earpiece with the other and then put it to her ear.

"It's too bad Jack doesn't share a room with Harry," she said as she jiggled the hook up and down. "Two in one room would be easier."

"Miss Margaret, that's brilliant!"

Maggie lowered the earpiece. "What's brilliant?"

"Two in one room!"

"You mean Jack and Harry?"

"Yes!" Meredith said, eagerly. "And we could put Parker and Mrs. Butters in there, too, if we can manage the stairs. Then we could keep an eye on everyone at once, and take proper turns with nursing and sleeping and—"

"We can't put Mrs. Butters and Parker in with my brothers!" Maggie looked as scandalized as if Meredith had suggested they go on holiday together.

"But—"

"But I suppose we could move Jack's mattress into Harry's room," Maggie said slowly, nodding. "Then we wouldn't have to move Jack. And I could stay with them both."

"But there'd still be Mrs. Butters downstairs and Parker upstairs," Meredith said. Maggie had seen how sick Mrs. Butters was. Maggie had even wondered what they'd do if Parker got sicker. Surely she understood how hard it would be to run up and down stairs all night?

Maggie shrugged. "We'll each have two. That's fair."

Meredith grabbed at another idea. "Could we move Parker downstairs, then?"

"You can move him if you like," Maggie said. "I'm not going up there ever again." She shuddered.

Meredith gritted her teeth. "I can't move him on my own," she said. "You know I can't."

Maggie turned back to the telephone. "We shouldn't be wasting time talking. I'm going to tell the hospital to send Forrest home. You start moving Jack's mattress." She put the earpiece in position without another glance at Meredith.

"Operator?" Maggie said loudly into the mouthpiece as she jiggled the hook. "Hello?"

Meredith trudged back up the stairs. Why did Jack have to go and get sick? It wasn't his fault, of course, but now he was one more worry when they had been stretched so thin already.

And Maggie wasn't going to listen to her. Meredith wondered whether Maggie would be any help at all.

CHAPTER 24

When Meredith reached Harry's room, she found the little boy arranging his lead soldiers into two lines on the floor beside his bed. "I stayed right here like you told me to," he said, puffing out his chest.

"You're a good helper," Meredith replied.

Jack appeared to be sleeping. She gently untied the soiled mask from around his neck and then used a towel she'd taken from the linen closet to remove the mess from his sweater. Being so close to him made her clumsy, however, and she dropped the towel onto his lap. As she snatched it up again, his eyes flew open much too close to hers. She swiped at the mess that had fallen on the floor, her face burning. She could feel Jack's eyes following her as she crossed the room.

"I'll be right back," she said to reassure both boys. She chucked the soiled towel onto the floor in the bathroom as she passed by. She'd put it in the laundry hamper later.

The walls of Jack's bedroom were papered with pictures of airplanes, their jaunty pilots wearing leather jackets and goggles. On a tall oak dresser, the biplane that Harry had snatched the day she arrived sat among a jumble of coins, playing cards, and wadded-up bits of paper. Other airplane models swung suspended from the ceiling. Meredith was certain Jack must have spent hours carefully cutting and neatly gluing the tiny pieces of wood.

His bed, however, looked as if a giant spoon had stirred the covers together. Meredith stripped its navy coverlet and white sheets, and bundled them onto the window seat.

"Why are you doing that?" Harry had followed her down the hall, a lead soldier in each fist.

"Oh, Mr. Harry! You need to stay with your brother."

"Maggie's there. I don't want her. I came to find you. Why are you doing that?"

"We're going to move the mattress so your brother can sleep in your room."

"Truly? In my room?" Harry asked, bouncing on his toes. "Why?"

"That way we can keep an eye on you both more easily."

"You'll have to be careful with that mattress," Maggie said crossly, appearing behind Harry. "Watch you don't hit the lamp."

"Maggie, Jack's going to sleep in my room!" Harry announced, pulling at Maggie's sleeve.

"You're in the way, Harry," Maggie said, shoving him aside.

"Ow!" Harry clutched his shoulder, and sudden tears threatened to spill over.

"You don't have to be so rough with him!" Meredith exclaimed, her heart beating double-time even though she had every right to stand up to Maggie. "He's only little, for heaven's sake, and he's still not feeling well."

Maggie opened her mouth, and then closed it again.

"His father's not here," Meredith went on, indignant on Harry's behalf, "and all he's got is you and your brother. Think about him for a minute!"

"You're not to talk to me..." Maggie began, but then she looked away. After a moment, she turned toward Harry. "Sorry," she said.

Harry edged away from his sister. "I wasn't in the way."

"I know," Maggie said. "I shouldn't have said that."

Harry looked at her solemnly, but he moved toward Meredith.

"Did you reach the doctor?" Meredith asked, hardly

daring to believe Maggie might have succeeded where Parker and Jack had failed.

Maggie shook her head. "I couldn't get through to an operator. I'll try again later."

Meredith surveyed the path to the door. "If you take that side, Miss Margaret, we can slide the mattress onto the floor."

"You're not expecting me to help move that mattress?"

"I can't do it on my own." Meredith looked steadily at the other girl.

"You can't do anything on your own, according to you," Maggie said. "You haven't even tried."

Meredith wanted to grab Maggie's arm and pinch it hard—she'd sure do that on her own—but it wouldn't get the mattress moved. She tried to keep her voice even. "I need your help with it, Miss Margaret."

"I can help!" Harry exclaimed from beside her.

Maggie ignored him. She narrowed her eyes at Meredith.

"Can't we just work together?" Meredith asked. She didn't want to beg, but she needed Maggie's help.

"I can work together." Harry hopped up and down beside Meredith. "I'm strong."

Maggie turned on him. "Don't be silly—" she began sharply, then she glanced at Meredith and sighed.

"That's good, Harry. We can use your help." She turned to Meredith. "I'll pull, you push. Harry, you come beside me."

Harry scrambled into place and grabbed hold of the corded edge of the mattress. He and Maggie pulled, Meredith pushed, and the mattress slid several inches toward Maggie and Harry.

"On three this time." Maggie braced her foot against the bed frame and counted. This time the mattress slid so far that she and Harry had to hop backward. Harry toppled onto the floor, laughing.

On the next try, the mattress whumped onto the floor. Harry cheered and even Maggie looked pleased.

Between them, the girls wrestled the floppy mattress onto its side and out the door. Harry scampered ahead as it lurched along the thick carpet, Maggie issuing instructions that Meredith mostly ignored.

It was like herding a large and balky cow, and Meredith was sweating by the time they propped the mattress against the doorframe of Harry's room to catch their breath. She pushed the curls that had come loose behind her ear.

Jack seemed to be asleep, but the rank smell in his room told them he'd been sick again. Meredith could see fresh vomit on his sweater. She hoped Mrs. Butters was all right downstairs. She'd need to check on her soon. Parker, too. What a mess it all was!

"Ready?" Maggie said. "We'll put it over by the window."

After they dragged the mattress into the room, Meredith stumbled over a small hooked rug at the foot of the bed and the edge of the mattress slipped out of her grasp. She figured they'd left enough space to move around the mattress, so she let it fall.

Maggie staggered as the weight of the mattress shifted toward her. "Over by the window, I said."

"It's far enough."

"I said put it by the window!"

"And *I* said it's far enough!" Meredith replied. Maggie didn't have to have it all her own way all the time.

"Oh, all right!" Maggie let the mattress drop onto the floor.

CHAPTER 25

All that remained was to move Jack onto the mattress.

"It will take both of us to get him there," Meredith said.

"But he's covered in…" Maggie screwed up her face. "I can't."

Meredith shoved her hands into the pockets of her apron. "Then I'm going downstairs. Mrs. Butters has been alone too long."

"You can't!" Maggie's anxious voice followed Meredith as she left the bedroom. "I'm in charge," Maggie said, running to catch up with Meredith in the hallway. "You have to do what I say. You can't just leave him there like that."

Meredith stopped at the top of the back stairs. "I'm doing exactly what you said, Miss Margaret. You said I was to look after Mrs. Butters and Parker." Meredith kept her voice steady. "You said you'd look after your family."

She'd reached the third step from the bottom when Maggie said, "Wait."

It wasn't Maggie's usual bossy tone.

"Wait, please."

Meredith looked up. Maggie's hair was a tangle on either side of her pale face. She didn't look sulky or even angry this time, she just looked worn out.

"I'll help," Maggie said. "Could you…could we get his sweater off? Then get him into his nightshirt? And then move him?"

"All right," Meredith said quietly. "But I'm going to check on Mrs. Butters first."

The old Maggie would have stormed and argued. This Maggie nodded. Meredith decided she liked this new one a whole lot better as she made her way to the back hall.

Thankfully, Mrs. Butters seemed to be all right despite the rasping noise that accompanied every rise of her chest. Meredith didn't know if it was worse than before, she only knew it was bad. They needed to find a way to get her to the hospital soon.

"It's about time," Maggie said when Meredith returned to Harry's bedroom. Harry was complaining loudly about the smell, holding his nose with one hand and arranging his soldiers into two lines with the other.

Meredith tugged her mask up over her nose and mouth; Maggie made a sour face, but she did the same.

Jack's eyes were glassy and he seemed confused. Getting his sweater off was like undressing one of Ellen's rag dolls grown life-sized. Maggie threaded his arms back through the sleeves, careful not to touch the vomit, while Meredith gathered the bottom of the sweater and eased it over his head. She was congratulating herself for containing the mess when some of it dripped onto Jack's bare chest.

"Eew! That's disgusting!" Maggie flinched. "I'll get his nightshirt." She fled before Meredith could argue.

Meredith couldn't help grimacing as she used Jack's sweater to mop up the mess, and her stomach was doing uneasy somersaults as she rolled the sweater into a ball and set it out in the hall. There'd be a mountain of laundry for Mrs. O'Hagan when this was all over.

With the sweater gone, Harry's room didn't smell quite so bad. Meredith hoisted the window to help freshen the air and bring down Jack's fever. She fetched a washcloth from the bathroom, and then wiped Jack's face and chest, trying not to catch his eye, but she was uncomfortably aware of his bare chest rising and falling below her arm.

"Good," he mumbled.

"What's good?" Meredith leaned closer to hear him better.

"That," he said. "Thanks."

She was sweating despite the open window. She hoped it was only being too close to him and not the first stirrings of the sickness in her. She'd been able to mostly avoid thinking about getting sick herself, but Jack falling ill with no warning had scared her. It was going to be harder to continue convincing herself that she'd somehow stay safe. A sudden lump in her throat made it hard to swallow.

"I don't know why you're just standing there," Maggie said impatiently, from the doorway. "We'll need to get his pants off, too."

Goodness! Meredith hadn't thought of his pants.

"Nightshirt first," Maggie said. She pulled it over Jack's head, and he grunted as she guided his arms through the sleeves. She tugged the nightshirt down over his chest. "His skin's awfully hot."

"It's the fever," Meredith said. "Mrs. Butters had it, too."

Maggie stood back and crossed her arms. "You do the pants."

Jack's naked chest had been disturbing enough; Meredith certainly didn't want to see him without his pants.

"Don't," Jack mumbled, shaking his head. "S'okay."

Meredith looked at Maggie.

Maggie tilted her head, considering. "Oh, all right," she conceded.

Getting Jack to stand was worse than wrestling his mattress. Movement made him dizzy. Even with a girl on each side, it took all the strength they had to keep him from collapsing back into the rocking chair.

"It's no use," Maggie said after what seemed like the twentieth try. "We need a sled or something."

The jumble of covers on Harry's mattress gave Meredith an idea. "What about a blanket? We could pull him over to the mattress on that."

"That might work." Maggie's eyes brightened. "That's clever, actually." Meredith thought Maggie might even be smiling at her from behind her mask.

Meredith lifted the blue wool blanket from Harry's bed and spread it on the floor in front of the rocking chair. Jack groaned as they eased him down onto the blanket. He looked younger to Meredith as he huddled there.

Maggie picked up one corner of the blanket and motioned to Meredith to take the other. "Together now," she said.

CHAPTER 26

For Meredith, the night that followed was a jumble of stairs and basins, wet cloths on foreheads, and trying to get first Mrs. Butters and then Parker to drink some water. More went in than dribbled out, and Meredith told herself that had to be a good sign. Still, she'd feel better when she and Maggie found a way to take them both to the hospital.

Parker turned his head away from the damp cloth Meredith was using to sponge his forehead as she sat with him in the early hours of the morning. The sun wasn't up yet, so the room felt dark and cramped. From time to time, Parker muttered words she couldn't make out. The memory of his blood-slick scalp in her hands did nasty things to her stomach, so she was careful to keep from touching his skin. Despite his fever, she was half-afraid his skin would feel cold and slippery like the skin of the plucked turkeys Uncle Dan brought to the store every Christmas.

She'd had no sleep at all. How delicious it would be to feel her bones melting into her own mattress, the welcome tide of sleep washing over her. She was tired of sick people and out of patience with it all. She sat back in the chair she'd dragged over from Parker's desk and closed her eyes.

Parker's muttering pulled her back from the edge of sleep. She set the basin of water on the bedside table beside a small black Bible with *D. B. Parker* stamped in gold on the front cover. She wondered what church he attended and whether he had friends there that he met up with sometimes, but it was impossible to imagine Parker having a life separate from Glenwaring.

Her eyes were drawn to a photograph in a silver frame on the dresser across the room, and she got up to examine it. In the photograph, Parker stood stiffly beside a man in uniform who looked like younger version of Parker, both men positioned behind an elderly woman who was seated in a chair. Parker rested his hand on the woman's shoulder; all three looked forbidding. Meredith knew their wooden expressions were the result of having to stay absolutely still for a long time so the photograph wouldn't blur, but even so, it was hard to picture any of them actually smiling.

She picked up the frame to take a closer look and a smaller photograph fluttered from the back onto the dresser. The young woman in this photograph wore a black straw hat with flowers the size of cabbages clustered on one side of the brim, and a long jacket with black braid and shiny buttons marching smartly down the front. Her skirt reached to her ankles, and her feet were turned out so you could see the stylish court heels on her shoes. Her gloved hands held a small pocketbook at her trim waist, and her eyes seemed to hold a smile for whoever was looking at her. Meredith couldn't resist turning the photograph over to search for a clue as to who she might be. An inscription in looping letters read, "*To dear Durward from Lydia. St. Ives, 1896.*"

It was ridiculous to think of Parker being anyone's "dear Durward," even if it had been years before she was born. Meredith wondered where St. Ives was, and whether Lydia might be Parker's sister, or even his sweetheart. Meredith couldn't picture that merry-looking young woman as the sweetheart of a dried-up stick like Parker.

You never know what troubles someone might have. Maybe Parker had a younger brother fighting somewhere in France? Maybe Lydia was a lost love? Maybe he hadn't always been like he was now; maybe things had happened to make him that way.

Parker's pale face was turned toward her, and she was worried for a moment that he'd caught her snooping, but to her relief he seemed to still be asleep. He wasn't wheezing like Mrs. Butters, so Meredith told herself they didn't need to watch him as closely as the others. He was bound to get sicker, and she dreaded the awful wheezing to come and the guck he'd cough up, but right now Mrs. Butters needed her more. She inched the window higher, then pulled the blanket up to Parker's chest and tucked it in neatly.

She could do that much for him, at least, on behalf of a sweetheart named Lydia or a brother overseas.

✚ ✚ ✚

The sour odor of unwashed bodies met Meredith at the doorway of Harry's room. The slight breeze stirring the lace curtains hadn't managed to entirely banish the smell. A tray on the dresser held the remains of Maggie's supper: a piece of bread, some crumbs of cheese and a half-eaten apple.

Harry was wrapped in a blanket and curled up like a kitten at the bottom of Jack's mattress. Maggie was kneeling beside Jack, trying in vain to sponge his forehead as his head rolled from side to side. His hair was plastered to his skull. Meredith could see he was much sicker than he'd been only a few hours ago.

"Stay still, Jack!" Maggie cried, sweating despite the cold. "It's no use at all if you don't stay still." She flung the cloth across the room where it splatted against a small oak dresser and then slowly slid to the ground.

Maggie sat back on her heels and caught sight of Meredith in the doorway. "Papa's got to come home," she said. "I've telephoned the hospital again and again, but mostly I don't get through, and when I do they say Papa is needed there and they'll give him the message, but I don't think they tell him anything at all."

"Tell them your brother is sick, desperately sick. Make it sound as if—" Meredith froze. In the sudden silence, Meredith could hear the soft sighing sound made by the edge of the lace curtain as the breeze brushed it across the low table under the window.

"Is that what you think?" Maggie asked, stricken. "That Jack might—"

"That's not what I meant," Meredith said quickly, even though they both knew it was. "Go telephone them now. I'll stay here."

Maggie nodded. She ran down the hall.

+++

Meredith stood at the doorway to Harry's room, listening hard. Maggie had been gone too long. At first, Meredith thought she hadn't been able to get through to the hospital, and then she thought it might be taking a long time to locate Dr. Waterton.

A noise from the front stairs caught her attention.

After a worried glance at the sleeping boys, she hurried along the hallway to the landing and looked over the railing to the front hall below.

Maggie sat on the bottom step rocking back and forth, her shoulders heaving, her hands pressed to her mouth.

Meredith raced down the stairs. "What's wrong?"

Maggie grabbed Meredith's hand and pulled her down onto the step beside her. "They said they couldn't get him," she sobbed, hanging on as if Meredith was a rope pulling her to safety. "I told them Jack was really sick, desperately sick like you said—" She took a gulping breath, "and they said there were people desperately sick there, too." She gulped for more air. "And then they gave me a number to call. To talk to a nurse."

It wasn't possible. No one was coming. There was no one to help.

"They said they'd try to find Forrest," Maggie continued. "But I don't think they will, and I don't know what to do!"

"Well, I do," Meredith said firmly. "Call the nurse."

"But Jack needs a doctor—"

"Listen to me," Meredith grabbed Maggie's other hand. "Your father will come just as soon as he gets the message."

"Do you really think so?"

"Yes, I do," Meredith said, hoping she sounded more confident than she felt. "I don't know why he hasn't got it yet. But you should call that nurse anyway. Maybe she can tell us something that will help. It's all we can do until someone comes."

Weariness had smudged dark circles under Maggie's eyes and her face was blotchy from crying. Meredith could no longer see any traces of the dainty doll in the lovely blue dress at Jack's party.

"And then you should rest," Meredith said firmly. "Have a nap, and then wash up. You'll feel better."

Maggie shook her head. "You can't manage all by yourself."

"I can stay with your brother for a little while," Meredith said, wishing now that she hadn't been so quick to offer. She'd be even more tired when Maggie reappeared. "But not for long. We've got to think about the others."

Maggie drew her hands back and slowly got to her feet. "I don't know why you're being nice to me," she said. "But I'll take a turn after so you can have a rest, too."

Meredith could only blink at her in surprise.

CHAPTER 27

Later that afternoon, the sunlight glinted gold in the long mirrors that stood opposite the tall windows in the drawing room. As she sat up, Meredith squinted at the glare, unsure for a moment where she was. When Maggie, looking much better, had relieved her earlier that morning, Meredith had been unable to banish the thought of Parker just down the hall from her bedroom. She'd ducked into the drawing room instead, wanting to be surrounded by something other than sickness for a little while. She'd intended to take only a short nap, but she must have slept for hours.

Meredith swung her feet off the blue-and-cream satin of the sofa. Mrs. Stinson would be horrified if she knew Meredith's feet had been resting on the Waterton's elegant furniture. The thought almost made Meredith laugh, but then she remembered Mrs. Butters and Parker and Jack. She hurried to the back hall.

Mrs. Butters was asleep, wheezing, her iron-gray hair snaked across the pillow. There was no sign of Maggie. Meredith hastily scrubbed at her face in the small bathroom off the back hall and bundled her greasy hair into a knot, wishing there was time for a proper wash. She ignored the dishes piled haphazardly in the kitchen sink and sped up the back stairs to find Maggie.

In Harry's room, Jack was sleeping, propped into a sitting position against the footboard of Harry's bed. Beside him, Harry's head poked out of a heap of covers on the mattress. His eyes were closed, too. It was a wonder either of them could sleep through the rasp of Jack's breathing.

Then Meredith made sense of what she'd thought was a heap of covers on the mattress: Maggie, mostly hidden under a blanket, curled around her little brother and sound asleep.

How long had Maggie had been asleep? Had she even bothered to check on Mrs. Butters or Parker? Meredith told herself she wouldn't have taken a nap if she'd thought Maggie was going to ignore them, but deep down she knew that wasn't true. She'd known all along that Maggie wouldn't go up to Parker, but the irresistible opportunity to get some sleep had been too strong. Maggie must have been as desperate for sleep as Meredith had been. Meredith couldn't blame her for that.

Seeing Maggie and Harry now, Meredith remembered how she'd curled around Ellen the same way, Ellen's solid little body spooned with hers in the bed they shared. Lying that way had comforted them both when Papa left them a lifetime ago. Maybe Maggie needed that kind of comfort now.

Meredith gently closed the bedroom door. Sleep was too precious to waste. Now that she was awake, Maggie might as well get whatever sleep she could.

Partway up the stairs to the third floor, the unmistakable sound of wheezing brought her to a standstill. She sank onto the step and burst into tears—fearing the worst, wanting to escape, missing Mama. Now *he'd* need to be propped up, kept from choking, watched closely so he wouldn't drown in the mucus filling his lungs. What a horrible mess it all was!

Meredith wrapped her arms around her knees and rocked there until the worst of the weeping passed. She wiped the tears from her wet cheeks and tried to think it all through.

First of all, Dr. Waterton couldn't have any idea about the chaos at Glenwaring or he'd have come straight home, especially with Jack so sick. Meredith knew that for a fact.

Second, even if the doctor hadn't known about Parker or Jack, he would have sent Forrest to check on them if he couldn't come himself. And Forrest would have done whatever Dr. Waterton asked. So something must have happened to Forrest. There was no point hoping he'd come and rescue them. Third, Maggie was right. If Dr. Waterton couldn't come to them, then their only hope was to somehow take Mrs. Butters and Jack and Parker to him.

It was up to her and Maggie to figure out how to do that.

Meredith got wearily to her feet and made her way to Parker's room. Up close, his wheezing didn't sound too bad. Mrs. Butters was much worse and she was hanging on. That meant they could concentrate on getting help for Mrs. Butters and Jack first, and could worry about Parker after.

She carried Parker's washbowl and jug to the cramped bathroom under the eaves where she emptied the bowl and refilled the jug with fresh water. Back in the bedroom, she found she couldn't maneuver Parker into a more upright position on her own, so for now she only wiped his face with the damp cloth. She curled one arm under his pillow and used the pillow to help raise his head to offer him some water, even though she hated being so close to him.

When the water touched his lips, Parker cried, "It's not the same!"

Startled, Meredith jerked back. Parker's head dropped onto the pillow. He cried out again as water sloshed out of the glass and across his face. It was clear he didn't know who she was or what was happening. When she put the glass to his lips again, most of the water dribbled out of the corners of his mouth and down his neck. She told herself it was all she could do for now, so she wiped her hands and headed back downstairs.

After checking on Mrs. Butters, Meredith was deciding whether she should tackle the dishes or hang up the masks that had been stewing in the copper boiler when she heard a knock at the back door. She hurried to answer it, hoping it was Forrest—even though she'd given up on him—and realizing in the same moment that Forrest wouldn't have knocked.

"Tommy!" Meredith's disappointment turned to pleasure when she saw him waiting on the porch. She stepped outside and closed the door behind her, then hugged her arms close against the chill morning. "I can't ask you in. We're not supposed to have visitors. Are you all right? How are your mum and your sisters?"

Tommy removed his cap. His face seemed thinner than Meredith remembered, his riot of freckles vivid against his pale skin.

"Are you hungry?" Meredith asked. "I could get you a plate of something."

"No," Tommy said, his hands twisting his cap. "No, thank you. I'm not hungry." His eyes didn't meet hers. They were like holes in the map of his face.

"Is it—" Meredith's throat closed over so she had to force the words out. "Is it Bernadette?"

Tommy shook his head. "No," he said, "Bernie's getting better."

Then she knew. "Your mama," she whispered.

Tommy nodded. He turned away. She could see the muscles in his jaw working.

"And then—yesterday—Mary." Tommy took an unsteady breath, but he held his body straight as if guarding himself from what was coming next. He seemed to be looking past Glenwaring, past Toronto even, all the way to some place Meredith couldn't see.

She hesitated, then reached out and touched his shoulder, but he moved away from her touch as if it burned him.

"We had a telegram yesterday," he said, the words so filled with pain that Meredith didn't want to hear the rest, but he plowed on. "Paddy's been killed. Mick's missing."

"Oh no!" Meredith searched for something she could say that might comfort him, but this loss was too big for words. When they'd received the news about Papa, Meredith had felt hollowed out for months, even though Mama had been there to help her bear the pain. But

Tommy had lost a mother, a sister and a brother all at once.

"You must eat something," she said at last. "You won't be any help to Bernadette if you get sick.

"Come sit in the kitchen," she said, opening the back door. Keeping Tommy outside was senseless after what he'd been through. "I'll get you something. It'll only take a minute."

She put the kettle on to boil, and then cut a thick slice of cheese and sandwiched it between two slabs of bread. When the tea was ready, she stirred two heaping spoons of sugar into his cup, thinking he needed it more than any soldiers. Mama always said that hot, sweet tea was the best thing for shock.

Although he'd said he wasn't hungry, Tommy tore into the sandwich and drained his cup, and Meredith was glad to see some color come back to his cheeks. She set about making a second sandwich.

"What will you do now?" she asked.

"I don't know," Tommy replied. "I don't even know why I came here. I wanted to yesterday, after...after Mary...but I couldn't leave Bernie, not after that."

Meredith imagined a little girl, crying, sitting alone on the floor beside a bed where two bodies lay. She was almost afraid to ask, but then the thought of what Tommy had faced gave her courage. "Your mama and Mary...are they at home?"

Tommy shook his head. "The undertakers came down our street last night." His voice caught, and he took a deep breath before continuing, "They call out and ring a bell so you can bring the…them…out in front of the house. We're lucky they came. Mrs. Hainey next door says some folks have waited two days or more."

He'd carried his mama and his sister out of the house all by himself so the undertakers could take them away. Meredith shuddered even as she marveled at how brave he'd been.

"I told Mrs. Hainey I was coming here this afternoon," Tommy went on. "She said Bernie could bang on the wall if she needed anything. Mrs. Hainey won't set foot in our house for fear of the flu, but she's been kind to us."

Meredith handed him the second sandwich wrapped in a napkin. Tommy tucked it into a pocket in his jacket.

"Thanks," he said. "I'll keep it for Bernie. Mrs. Hainey brings us soup from St. Patrick's and leaves it on the step, but Bernie's awfully tired of soup."

"Who's Bernie? And who are you?"

Maggie stood just inside the door from the hallway, her hands on her hips, her hair tangled about her face. "We're not supposed to have visitors," Maggie went on, "although I don't know that it matters anymore."

"I'm sorry, miss," Tommy said, getting to his feet. "I'll be on my way."

"Wait!" Meredith exclaimed. She couldn't bear to think of Bernie and Tommy all alone in the cheerless house where their family had died. "I've got an idea."

As Tommy stood by, Meredith explained to Maggie about Tommy and his family. Several times while she was speaking, Tommy looked as if he wanted to say something, but he only shifted from foot to foot and kept his eyes on the cap in his hands.

"All of them?" Maggie looked at Tommy, eyes wide.

Meredith nodded. "Except for Bernie, and she's getting better." She took a deep breath. "What if they came to stay here?"

Tommy looked up at that. "I didn't come for charity," he protested. He turned toward Meredith. "I know you're only trying to help, but—"

"It's out of the question," Maggie said firmly. "We've got our hands full as it is."

"But that's just it," Meredith said eagerly. "It wouldn't be charity, and it would help us. Tommy can help with laundry, and meals, and fetch coal, and—"

"What about his sister?" Maggie broke in. "Won't she need looking after?"

"She's on the mend. She could play with Harry. He's feeling so much better, and it's hard for us to keep an eye on him now."

"But what if she gets sick again? Or he does?"

Maggie motioned toward Tommy. "It'd mean more work, not less."

"The newspaper hasn't reported anyone getting sick a second time," Meredith said. "And Tommy's like you and me: he stayed healthy while everyone around him was getting sick."

Maggie frowned.

Meredith grabbed at another idea. "You could even send Tommy to the hospital," she said, "to take a message to your father. Tommy would find a way to deliver it in person."

Maggie blinked. "I hadn't thought of that."

"You said yourself it's too much, all of this, for just you and me," Meredith plowed on. "There's even an empty bedroom on the third floor. It's perfect."

"It *would* be good to have help," Maggie said slowly. "All right. For now. Until Papa comes."

Meredith felt as if she'd surged across the finish line of a footrace, only the prize for this was better than any ribbon. They'd finally have the help they so desperately needed.

"So I'm to bring Bernie here?" Tommy looked at Maggie as if she'd suddenly started speaking another language. "We're to stay here? In this house?"

"I just said so, didn't I?" Maggie looked cross. "But don't think it's going to be a holiday."

"Thank you, miss!" Tommy crossed the floor and grabbed Maggie's hand. He shook it as though he were manning a pump for the fire brigade. "I'm a hard worker, and Bernie will be no trouble. You won't be sorry."

CHAPTER 28

After Tommy left, Meredith washed the dishes and hung the tea towel to dry on the rack by the range. The quiet in the kitchen unsettled her. Before the Spanish Flu, Forrest might have been coming in from outside, stamping his feet on the mat, while Jack clattered in from the hall and Harry lurked near the sugar bowl.

Never mind, Meredith told herself. Tommy would be back soon with Bernadette. Then there'd be noise and, best of all, help.

Meredith set a pot of water to boil, and then fetched the tub of oatmeal and a box of raisins from the pantry. Harry might manage porridge for his supper if she sugared it well. She could make a face on top with raisins like she'd done for Ellen at home, back when there'd been money for raisins.

She leaned against the counter as she waited for the water to boil. When Mama made porridge, the chipped lid of the white enamel pot would rattle cheerfully as the water bubbled. Ellen would hop around the kitchen, singing in her funny way as she set the table. Mama would spoon the steaming porridge into three blue-and-white striped bowls, sprinkling Ellen's and Meredith's with precious brown sugar while only pretending to sprinkle some on her own.

Meredith stirred the oatmeal vigorously into the boiling water, the spoon knocking against the sides of the pot. Memories of the cozy kitchen in Port Stuart made her miss home too much. It was better to keep busy.

The kitchen clock had stopped sometime in the night, so there was no friendly *tick-tock* to keep her company. The only sound from outside was the faint *chick-a-dee-dee-dee* of the little birds she could see hopping from branch to branch in the rosebushes under the kitchen window. She couldn't remember when it had last been this quiet; Mrs. Butters' noisy wheezing had become a constant accompaniment to everything she did.

There was no accompaniment now.

The wooden spoon clattered into the pot as Meredith rushed to Mrs. Butters' side. Her eyes fastened on the rough wool blanket over the cook's chest. She sank to the floor beside the settee.

"Mrs. Butters!" She stretched her hand out, and then drew it back again, afraid her fingers might discover something other than everything being all right.

The cook's eyelids fluttered open. "Ben?" Her voice was like a rusty gate.

"It's me, Mrs. Butters! Meredith!" She grabbed Mrs. Butters' hand, warm as fresh-baked bread, not burning with fever.

"Where's Ben?" Mrs. Butters peered at Meredith. Close up, Meredith could still hear a wheeze, but nothing like before.

"Ben's in France, Mrs. Butters. He's fine. You're fine." She squeezed the cook's hand. "You've been so sick." The words tripped over each other. "How do you feel? Do you want some water? Are you hungry?"

Mrs. Butters coughed, a rattle that shook her body and threatened to go on and on. Meredith slid her arm across the cook's back and eased her forward as she groped for the basin on the floor beside the settee. She thumped Mrs. Butters' back as the cook coughed up horrible, yellow-green stuff that fell into the basin. When the coughing ended, Meredith listened anxiously as Mrs. Butters' breathing settled down to even breaths, not jagged ones, and much less wheezing.

"Water?" Mrs. Butters whispered.

Meredith ran to the kitchen tap and filled a glass.

Her hands shook so much that she slopped water onto the floor as she carried it back. Mrs. Butters sucked at the water, and then drew her head back from the glass.

"Good," Mrs. Butters murmured.

"It's better than good! It's wonderful!" Meredith smoothed Mrs. Butters' hair, and then briefly touched the back of her hand to Mrs. Butters' forehead. "Your fever's broken," she whispered. "I think you're going to be fine."

Mrs. Butters' black button eyes looked up, straight into Meredith's. "Good girl," she whispered.

+++

Meredith had raced upstairs to tell Maggie the good news about Mrs. Butters, but now she hesitated at the doorway to Harry's room. Maggie and Harry were playing Snakes and Ladders at the small table under the window while Jack slept, the sound of his labored breathing filling the room. Harry crowed as Maggie slid her token down a long snake, and Maggie looked happier than she had in days. Neither had spotted her, so Meredith left them to have their fun. Her good news would keep.

She trudged upstairs and looked in on Parker, who seemed to be sleeping quietly. She was jangly with excitement over Mrs. Butters, too unsettled to remain with Parker, glad to leave him undisturbed for the time being.

She decided to wait for Tommy outside, so she hastened down the stairs and only just remembered to take the pot of porridge off the stove. She slipped out the back door, waving to a dozing Mrs. Butters.

The late afternoon sun made her blink after so much time inside. She filled her lungs with fresh air scented by the few remaining roses. Whistling, she walked around to the front of the house and down the driveway to the stone gatepost. When she'd first arrived, the graceful letters chiseled there seemed to mean elegant and wonderful, but they'd turned out to mean nothing but work and worry.

The newspaper had been delivered to the gate. There it was again—the headline "Yesterday's Dead"—posted over a grim list of the names and addresses of the people in Toronto who'd died from the Spanish Flu the day before, the same way the paper listed the names of soldiers who'd died overseas. It seemed to her that the Spanish Flu was like an invading army, leaving grief in its wake as it spewed casualties.

But Mrs. Butters wasn't a casualty, she reminded herself. Mrs. Butters was getting better.

Would Jack? Would Parker?

Meredith swung her arms to help shake away the dark thoughts until the swinging started her twirling and the twirling made her dizzy. She wanted to be dizzy. She wanted to spin around so fast that she'd shoot up through the trees and soar over Toronto, following the train tracks all the way to Port Stuart.

"Look, Bernie! A dancing fairy!"

Meredith grabbed the gatepost. When the world stopped whirling, she saw Tommy towing a wagon piled with bedding. A pink knitted hat was pulled right down to the eyebrows of a small, white face peeking out of the pile like a cherry on a cupcake.

"It's not," said the person under the hat. "It's a girl."

"It's a fairy in disguise," Tommy said.

"It's a rotten disguise," Meredith said as they drew to a stop in front of her. "Fairies don't do kitchen work."

"Kitchen work or not, you're the Good Fairy for Bernie and me." Tommy lifted his sister. The quilt she'd been wrapped in fell back into the wagon.

"You're a load of bricks, Bernie!" he exclaimed. "You'll have to walk."

Bernie shook her head and then buried her face in his shoulder. Tommy hiked her higher in his arms and sighed.

"Never mind," Meredith said. "We're only going as far as the kitchen for now."

"Good thing." Tommy followed Meredith around the back of the house, grunting a little from the effort of carrying his sister.

"I've got a surprise," Meredith said when they

reached the back door, pleased to see Bernie's head bob up in response.

Mrs. Butters was awake, her face brightening when she caught sight of Tommy and Bernie, but then she was seized by a fit of coughing.

"Water," she croaked. Meredith hurried to the kitchen.

"Sit down," Mrs. Butters gasped, once the coughing subsided and she'd swallowed some water. Tommy perched on the chair beside the settee with Bernie on his lap. Meredith bent to help Mrs. Butters sit more upright when a bell began ringing furiously from upstairs.

"Go," Mrs. Butters urged, but Meredith was already running for thc stairs.

When she reached Harry's room, a white-faced Harry was perched at the end of his bed, frantically ringing a little brass bell. On the mattress below, Maggie was straining to keep Jack propped up while his arms and legs mashed the bedclothes. Jack's strangled breathing ripped at the air.

"Breathe!" Maggie urged. Strands of her hair, dark with sweat, stuck to her cheeks. "You have to breathe!"

Jack's face was the purple-red of overripe plums, his eyes distended like those of Mrs. Butters in one of her coughing fits.

Meredith ran to Maggie's side, but then Tommy

elbowed past her and fell to his knees beside Jack. He shoved Jack forward and began pounding him on the back.

"Stop!" Maggie cried, slapping at Tommy's arms. "You'll hurt him!"

"No!" Meredith pulled her back. "It'll help. You'll see."

Maggie watched uncertainly for a moment, and then she shook off Meredith's restraining hand. She scrambled into a position in front of Jack and pulled him toward her, propping his chin on her shoulder and exposing more of his back.

"Keep going!" she cried when Tommy stopped, his fist in mid-air.

Maggie winced at each blow, but she held on. Meredith put her arms around a whimpering Harry, watching in horror as Jack fought to breathe.

One more breath, Meredith prayed with each thump, *one more breath*, until Jack, gagging, expelled a wad of something onto Maggie's shoulder. Maggie recoiled at that, but she didn't let go. Tommy's arm hovered uncertainly, but then Jack drew a great shuddering breath that seemed to suck all the air out of the room.

Tommy sat back on his heels, panting. His eyes sought Meredith's as Maggie eased her brother back against the footboard of the bed. Jack's eyes were glassy, but he was breathing.

Maggie pushed his wet hair back from his forehead.

"You're all right," she said softly. "Just breathe, Jack."

"Is—is Jack going to die?" Harry's lip trembled as he looked up at Meredith.

Meredith blinked away the threat of tears. "No," she said when she could speak again. "He's doing better now. They helped him."

"You saved him," Maggie said to Tommy.

Tommy ran his hand through his hair, leaving it sticking up like a rooster's comb. "I hope you won't mind me saying, miss, but Mam—" his voice caught, "my mama was sick just like that. He needs to be in hospital."

"I know that," Maggie said shakily. "I've said that all along, but a taxi won't take someone who's sick, so we've been waiting for Forrest—"

"Except we think something must have happened to Forrest," Meredith broke in. "We need another plan."

"Begging your pardon, miss," Tommy said, but including Meredith in his gaze, "you can't wait any longer. You need to take him now."

That started Harry wailing. Jack began another scraping breath, pulling Meredith's eyes to him as she hugged Harry close.

"I know that!" Maggie cried. "I know all of that, but I don't know how to get him there." She looked utterly spent.

Tommy's eyes traveled from Maggie to her brother.

"Then I'll take him," Tommy declared. "I'll get him to the hospital, miss, even if I have to carry him there myself."

To Meredith, it was as if Tommy's words had pushed aside the heavy velvet curtains at the window and sunlight was flooding in. "But you don't have to carry him!" she cried. "You can use the wagon."

She turned to Maggie. "Tommy brought his sister here in a wagon."

"Did you hear that, Jack?" Maggie asked, her face brightening. "We're taking you to the hospital! In a wagon!"

Between them, Tommy and Meredith carried Jack downstairs, Maggie hovering beside them carrying blankets, Harry trailing behind. It was heavy going, and Meredith's arms ached from the strain. Once they reached the back hall, Harry rushed to Mrs. Butters' side to tell her the news. She put an arm around him as Bernie watched from the end of the settee, big-eyed and silent.

As they maneuvered him outside to the waiting wagon, Jack cried out if they jostled him too much. Meredith wondered if he knew what was happening as Maggie and Tommy wedged him into the wagon, his feet tucked inside the front edge, his knees sticking straight up. Maggie swathed him in the blankets she'd ferried outside as she gave Tommy instructions about what to say when he reached the hospital.

Tommy hauled on the handle and the wagon lurched behind him. "He's a lot heavier than Bernie," he said.

"It's Toronto City Hospital, remember. Ask for Dr. Waterton," Maggie reminded him.

Meredith hugged her arms against the cold as she and Maggie stood watching the wagon's progress down the path. Jack began to gasp and splutter even before the wagon reached the street. Tommy dropped the handle and immediately began thumping him on the back as Maggie raced down the steps, Meredith close behind her. They held Jack upright, not daring to look at each other, while Tommy worked to clear the mucus from his lungs.

"It's no use," Maggie said, despairing, once Jack quieted again. "It's three miles to the hospital at least. How long will it take if you have to stop every five minutes because he can't breathe?"

"I'll stop every *two* minutes if need be," Tommy declared. "I told you I'd take him to the hospital, and that's what I'm going to do."

"He won't have to stop, Miss Maggie," Meredith said, "not if you go with him. I can manage here."

The sound of an approaching automobile made them all turn their heads. Meredith prayed it was Forrest, prayed the car would turn into the driveway, even though she knew she'd be disappointed like all the other times she'd hoped it was him. She'd given up hoping for miracles.

But this automobile turned in at the gate and jolted to a sudden stop. The driver flung the door open and hurried around the front of the car.

"Papa!" Maggie cried.

"Jack!" Dr. Waterton raced to the wagon.

CHAPTER 29

Maggie threw her arms around her father as he bent over Jack. Tears streamed down her face as she babbled a confused account of Jack's illness. Meredith could hardly believe it was really the doctor at last. Maggie jabbered on about Parker, along with the good news about Harry and Mrs. Butters.

After a quick examination, the doctor beckoned to Tommy, and they bundled Jack into a sitting position in the back seat of the car. Maggie tried to slide in beside her brother.

Dr. Waterton held her back. "No, Maggie," he said firmly.

"But I can help—"

"No 'buts,'" he said. "There isn't time to argue. I'll see

to Jack. Harry needs you here." He turned to Meredith. "Can Parker wait until I return?"

"I think so, sir. He's not so bad as—"

Just then, Jack erupted in a fit of choking. Tommy slid onto the back seat of the car and began pounding his back.

"Stay right there," Dr. Waterton said to Tommy. "I'll take you with me."

"No!" Maggie shrieked as the doctor slammed the car door and hurried around to the driver's seat. "Take me, Papa!"

The engine growled to life. The long, black automobile started down the driveway and pulled out through the gateposts into the street, trailing a cloud of exhaust.

The back door banged behind Maggie as Meredith stood shivering in the driveway watching the car get smaller and smaller until it finally disappeared around a corner.

✚✚✚

"You're supposed to attack, Bernie!" Harry's exasperated voice came from the pantry. "That's what armies do!" Harry's soldiers were keeping him and Bernie busy while Mrs. Butters napped.

Meredith was sweeping the kitchen floor as vigorously as if she were one of Harry's soldiers attacking it. It had been several hours since Dr. Waterton had taken

Jack to the hospital and there'd been no word yet. She'd knocked on the closed door of Maggie's bedroom before supper, but all she received in reply was a muffled "Go away!" She hadn't seen Maggie since, but she imagined that Maggie was praying just as hard as she was for Jack to pull through.

"Meredith!" Mrs. Butters called.

Meredith set the broom down and hurried to the back hall where she found Mrs. Butters standing beside the settee, clutching a blanket around her and smiling broadly at Meredith's surprise. "Help me to my chair," she said breathlessly.

"You should be resting," Meredith scolded. Nevertheless, she held her arm out for the cook to lean on.

"All I've done is rest," Mrs. Butters said with some of her old spark, clutching Meredith's arm, "and lying there worrying isn't doing me any good. Any word about Jack?"

"Not yet." Meredith matched her steps to Mrs. Butters' halting shuffle.

"Poor lad," Mrs. Butters said, leaning more heavily on Meredith as they entered the kitchen.

Meredith tried not to mind the sour smell wafting from Mrs. Butters' clothing. She hadn't had a bath or even a proper wash since she'd fallen ill. Meredith hugged the cook's arm close, grateful for her solid warmth.

Mrs. Butters was panting by the time she sank into

her usual chair at one end of the kitchen table, her cheeks flushed.

"It's as good as a holiday to be out of that dreary hall!" she exclaimed between wheezy breaths as Meredith hurried to the sink for some water.

"Come on, Bernie." Harry towed the little girl behind him out of the pantry. He stopped, eyes round, at the sight of Mrs. Butters in her chair.

"Are you better now?" he asked. He seemed shy, as if this Mrs. Butters, wrapped in a blanket with her hair undone down her back, would take some getting used to.

"Much better," Mrs. Butters replied. "But Bernadette looks tired."

"Bernie says her soldiers are tired." Harry pouted. "I told her soldiers don't get tired."

"Everyone gets tired," Mrs. Butters said solemnly, although Meredith could see a smile threatening. "Soldiering is hard work."

"I'm not tired," Harry said.

"You're not a soldier," said a small voice.

"Good gracious!" Mrs. Butters clapped her hands together. "Was that Miss Bernadette O'Hagan?"

Bernie nodded, trying to hide a smile.

"Then you must be feeling better," Mrs. Butters said to her. "That's very good news."

Bernie ducked behind Harry. "Let's go," she said. "My

soldiers are rested now."

Harry wheeled and raced for the pantry. "Atta-a-a-ck!" he cried.

Meredith and Mrs. Butters laughed as Bernie trailed after him.

"Are you sure you should be sitting up like this?" Meredith asked when they could hear the battle underway once more.

"I'm fine," Mrs. Butters assured her. "Hadn't you better check on Parker?"

✚✚✚

Parker lay on the narrow bed, his face turned toward the wall, the blue coverlet tidily pulled up over his chest. Meredith filled the wash basin with fresh water, and then set it on the floor beside the bed. She dragged the wooden chair closer to the bed and sat down, pulling her sweater around her against the draft from the open window. She took a cloth from the basin, wrung the water out of it and lifted it toward Parker's forehead.

Parker's half-open eyes stared unblinking at the ivy twining up the wallpaper. His jaw hung slack. His chest was still.

Meredith's heart pounded. She grabbed the edge of the mattress to steady herself.

Dead.

Parker was dead. Not a person anymore; a carcass to be hauled away like one of Uncle Dan's dead hogs.

He hadn't been as sick as the others. She'd left him alone all day.

Now he'd died.

The floor seemed to fall away beneath her. She swayed and collapsed against the back of Parker's chair. As the woozy feeling began to ebb and the edges of the room came back into focus, Meredith's eyes fastened on the small black Bible on the table by his bed. Had Parker ever turned to it for comfort, the way she did sometimes? Were there passages he'd known by heart? Had it been a gift from the family in the silver frame on the dresser? From a sweetheart whose picture he'd tucked in behind?

She hadn't known the first thing about him. She hadn't cared to know. Now she never would.

"You're not sick, are you?" Maggie's voice came from the doorway. "Mrs. Butters was worried."

"No. It's just—"

"Just what?"

Meredith rose unsteadily from the chair. Her foot upended the wash basin. Water sloshed over her battered leather shoes and across the bare wooden floor.

"Parker is dead," she said carefully, the words strange in her mouth.

"Oh no!" Maggie backed into the hallway.

Meredith followed, minding very much that her shoes were wet, thinking at the same time that it wasn't right to be worrying about something as ordinary as wet shoes. She leaned against the wall, grateful for something to hold her up. "I thought he was sleeping," she said slowly.

"I didn't think of him at all," Maggie whispered. The thin light from the electric fixture overhead gave her pale face a papery look. Blank-eyed, she leaned against the wall beside Meredith. "I was supposed to be in charge."

Meredith wondered if Maggie's heart was racing as fast as her own. "Listen to me," She said. She groped for Maggie's hand, for the comfort of someone to hold on to, surprised when Maggie's fingers gripped hers fiercely. "Your brother might have died if you hadn't been with him. You kept him safe until your father got here. That's the honest-to-goodness truth."

"None of that helped Parker," Maggie whispered.

"Yesterday you asked me what would happen if Parker got worse," Meredith said, working it out as she said it, plowing ahead to find the meaning in it. "Well, that's what happened. He got worse. Parker—" her mouth stumbled over the awfulness of what had happened to Parker. She paused so she'd get the words just right.

"We did the best we could," she said at last.

After a long moment, Maggie drew a deep, shuddering breath. She nodded.

From where they stood, Meredith could see the waning moon suspended in the square of blue-black sky framed by the window at the end of the hall. She pointed, and Maggie turned her face toward it. They stood like that, hands clasped together in the silent hallway, looking at the moon until the ringing of the telephone sent them running down the stairs.

✚ ✚ ✚

Meredith could hear Bernie reading haltingly to Harry, the two of them snug under a blanket on the settee in the back hall. She quietly relayed to Mrs. Butters Dr. Waterton's telephone message that Jack was now under the care of nurses at the hospital, and then explained about Parker. Maggie stood beside her, stone-faced. She hadn't spoken since talking to her father.

"Oh, my stars!" Mrs. Butters sat in her chair looking from one girl to the other, her hand fanning her face. "The poor man. Such a sad, sad thing."

She reached for Maggie's hand, and then Meredith's. "We'll mourn Parker, of course we will, but we can be thankful, too, that Mr. Jack has every chance of getting better now."

Meredith saw Maggie relax a little at Mrs. Butters' words.

Thankful was only one part of what Meredith was

feeling. Parker hadn't been the enemy she'd painted him. He'd just been a man with a family and sorrows in his past, his life cut off before he'd finished it.

She wished she'd known it would turn out like that.

CHAPTER 30

Something *had* happened to Forrest, just as Meredith had suspected. He'd fallen ill while helping transport patients and had been taken to one of the hotels that the city had commandeered as makeshift hospitals. In the confusion with so many people sick and dying, no one made the connection between him and Dr. Waterton until several days had passed.

Both Forrest and Jack had remained in hospital for weeks, but now it was late November and they were back at Glenwaring. The long job of convalescence had begun. Mrs. Butters had returned home, taking Bernie and Tommy to stay with her, but she came to Glenwaring every day to supervise a thorough cleaning of the house, determined to banish any lingering germs.

"I was just telling Tommy to start on the library today," Mrs. Butters announced one morning when she and Tommy arrived after delivering Bernie at school. She unpinned her hat and surveyed the kitchen.

Meredith was finishing up the breakfast dishes as Forrest read aloud snippets from the newspaper. Peace had been declared only the week before and Forrest liked to read out accounts of what that meant in Europe and at home.

Although seventeen hundred people in Toronto had died from the Spanish Flu, the worst of the outbreak was over and the city was slowly returning to normal. The illness was creeping westward across Canada, but Forrest wouldn't read aloud accounts of the continuing devastation. He'd told Meredith the newspaper wasn't going to tell them anything they didn't already know about the Spanish Flu, and that they should focus on the future instead.

"More dusting," Tommy said cheerfully as he and Meredith made their way to the library, carrying a broom, dustpan, and a bag of dusting cloths. Over weeks of working together, Meredith's admiration for Tommy had grown. She knew it must be difficult for him to be here where his mother had been employed for so many years, but he never complained, even with all he'd lost, and he always found some way to make their chores fun. Harry adored him and was much easier to manage when Tommy was around. Meredith didn't even mind the endless dish-washing because Tommy made her laugh so hard as he dried them.

They found Jack sprawled glumly in the big leather chair behind the desk in the library. Harry and Bernie had eagerly returned to their reopened schools; a subdued Maggie had been less enthusiastic, but she faithfully collected Jack's assignments from his school since he wasn't yet well enough to return to classes. Jack was staring into space, a large book open on his lap.

"We're to air out the library," Meredith announced.

Jack made a face. "I'll move then," he said, although he didn't budge.

"No need," Tommy said. "We can work around you. We get pretty tired of our own company."

"At least you have company," Jack muttered. Meredith thought he must feel rootless rattling around the house all day on his own.

"I do," Tommy said, "but I can always use more." He positioned the wooden library stool in front of one of the bookcases that flanked the fireplace. He stuffed a couple of dusting cloths in his pocket and stepped up onto the stool.

"I'm not good company today." Jack's eyes were on the book in his lap. One leg kicked at the desk, while the fingers of one hand traced the edge of the book.

Meredith had started removing books from the lower

shelf of the bookcase on the other side of the fireplace and piling them on the floor. She glanced at Jack, troubled, but he was scowling and she thought it best to leave him to his own thoughts.

Tommy began whistling "Alexander's Ragtime Band" as he pulled books off the top shelf and dusted them. Meredith eagerly joined in, trying to harmonize to his melody, but she kept losing her place and they were soon laughing at the awful combination of sounds they made.

"I'm sorry," Meredith said, turning to Jack, "You must think we've gone crazy. And we're keeping you from reading."

Jack shook his head. "It's good to hear someone having fun. This isn't very interesting anyway." He closed the book with a bang and dropped it onto the desk.

"Aeroplane Construction and Operation," Meredith read the title out loud and then looked up at Jack, puzzled. "But you want to be a pilot. Isn't this just the sort of book you'd love?"

Tommy hopped down from the stool and leaned across the desk to read the secondary title, "*A Comprehensive Illustrated Manual of Instruction for Aeroplane Constructors, Aviators, Aero-Mechanics, Flight Officers and Students.*" He ran his hand through his hair. "Whew! That's impressive."

"Not any more. The doctors said I can't be a pilot. My lungs won't be strong enough for the thin air." Jack was gaunt since he'd come out of hospital. Mrs. Butters worried that he needed to build up his strength.

"That's horrible," Meredith said quietly. She knew it was hard to give up a dream. She hoped she wouldn't have to give up becoming a teacher, but she didn't see how she was to manage it.

"That's tough all right," Tommy said. "What are you going to do?"

"I'm not sure," Jack said. "I met a lot of soldiers in the hospital. Some with bad wounds, some with bad lungs from the flu or mustard gas, others not right in the head. It made me think, seeing them all like that. Now that the war is over, some of them might be able to go back to the life they had before, but others won't. The war changed everything for them."

"And not just for the soldiers," Meredith said, looking at Tommy, "but for their families, and everyone around them. Just like the Spanish Flu did."

"I guess they're going to need doctors when they all come home," Jack went on, with a hint of his old smile, "since I can't be Billy Bishop now, or even the Red Baron."

Meredith remembered the conversation they'd had on the back step before his birthday party. He'd sounded so certain about his future then. Now all the money in the world couldn't buy him what he wanted, no matter how badly he wanted it.

Nothing could bring Tommy's family back, either. And the Spanish Flu had killed Parker.

But Jack and Tommy were alive, with a future in front of them. It was up to them—up to all of them—to make the most of it.

"You'd be a good doctor," Meredith said to Jack, and she meant it. She vowed that someday she'd be a good teacher, too.

CHAPTER 31

"There she is!" Meredith leapt to her feet and waved as the train pulled into the station at Port Stuart. When the train stopped, she jolted against the seat in front and nearly lost her balance. "See, Bernie? The woman in the gray hat with the little girl beside her. Mama! Ellen! Here I am!"

Mama and Ellen couldn't hear her, of course, and now the clouds of steam that curled over the snow-covered platform hid them from view. Meredith tucked her poetry book into the pocket of her dress and shrugged into her coat. She felt as if fireworks were about to go off inside her any second.

"Do you think they'll like me?" Bernie asked from the seat beside her.

In her eagerness to see her family, Meredith had forgotten that Bernie might be shy. She took Bernie's hand. "Mama's going to love you, and Ellen will, too."

Bernie looked to her brother who was watching them from across the aisle.

"Put your coat on, Bernie," Tommy said. "I've got our bag." He reached for Meredith's battered suitcase, too.

Meredith was glad all over again she was wearing her new coat of dove-gray wool with the rabbit fur on the collar. Glad, too, for the new hat and gloves from Mrs. Butters. She felt a million times more grown up than the girl who'd left Port Stuart three months ago.

"I can't wait for them to meet you," Meredith said, leading the way down the aisle. She'd been overjoyed when Mama suggested that Tommy and Bernadette come for Christmas. It was just what they needed after such a sad time.

Meredith paused at the top of the steps that led to the platform. She wanted to stretch this moment out so she'd always remember Mama's eager face searching for her among the passengers leaving the train.

But then she couldn't wait one second longer. She ran down the steps, breathing in the scents of home: smoke from the engine, horses with their sleighs alongside the platform. Harness bells jingled a welcome as drivers loaded their sleighs with parcels and passengers.

"There she is!" Ellen cried. She raced along the platform, blue hat bobbing, and barreled into Meredith. "Merry, Merry, I've missed you so much." Her tight hug made Meredith gasp, but she hugged Ellen back just as fiercely.

"That's a new hat," Meredith said, tweaking her sister's freckled nose.

"It's from Aunt Jane," Ellen said. Mama and Ellen had escaped the Spanish Flu, but Mama hadn't written about Aunt Jane until after the danger had passed. Her lively description of Aunt Jane's grouchy recovery had made Meredith laugh out loud in her bedroom at Glenwaring.

"She said she might as well knit if she had to stay in bed. She made you a red one. Oh, no!" Ellen's eyes grew round. "I wasn't supposed to tell!"

And then there was only Mama's smiling face and her arms flung wide. "My good girl," Mama said, reaching over Ellen to gather Meredith close.

More than the familiar sounds and smells of Port Stuart, Mama's scent of talcum and roses—the smell of hugs and goodnight kisses for as far back as Meredith could remember—told Meredith she was home at last. She hadn't expected Mama's tears, or her own.

"I can scarcely believe how grown-up you look," Mama said, crying and laughing as she held Meredith at arms' length. "I'm so proud of you!" She rummaged in her pocketbook for a handkerchief.

"You need to meet Tommy and Bernadette," Meredith said, wiping her eyes before beckoning them over. Bernie hung back, suddenly shy, but Tommy nudged her forward.

Mama knelt down in front of Bernadette. "Hello, my dear. We're very glad you've come to visit."

Beside her, Ellen squirmed with impatience. "Tinks had kittens, five of them," she announced. "Do you want to see?"

Bernie twisted around to look up at her brother.

"It's all right," Tommy said, patting her shoulder. "Go on."

"You girls can run on ahead," said Mama.

Ellen grabbed Bernie's hand and pulled her along the boardwalk. Mrs. Butters had fussed over Bernie, and Forrest made up silly stories to make her laugh, but Meredith thought a dose of Ellen was just what Bernie needed to chase the shadows from her pale face.

"And here's Tommy, of course," Mama said, extending her hand. "I'm so sorry for your loss, my dear," she said, her warm voice wrapping around him like a hug as they shook hands. "We've been so looking forward to your visit. It's making Christmas extra special for us."

"I don't know how to thank you," Tommy said, his voice catching. He had worked hard to be cheerful for

Bernie's sake, and he never complained, but Meredith knew he ached for his family. "Bernie hasn't been able to talk of anything else for days."

"There are no thanks needed," Mama said, "but if you've a mind to, I could use your help at the store. It's a busy time of year."

"Anything!" Tommy said.

It was just like Mama to make Tommy feel needed. "Tell her your news," Meredith suggested. She had her own news to share, but she was saving it for Christmas Day.

"I'm getting cold standing here," Mama said. "We can walk and talk at the same time. Good news, I hope?"

"The best," Tommy said, picking up the suitcases. They set off along the snow-covered sidewalk, Mama keeping pace with Tommy, Meredith trailing behind. She wanted to savor every little detail: a smart black hat sporting a spray of holly in the window of Miss Beadle's millinery, the line of waiting men framed by the steamy barbershop window, the new lace curtains at the manse.

"A letter came yesterday," Tommy said. "My brother Mick has turned up in England." Mick's letter had been read and re-read so often over the last twenty-four hours that Meredith was sure Tommy could recite it by heart.

"He'd been wounded and got separated from his unit," Tommy explained. "Someone had looted his kit, so he had no papers when an English unit found him. They knew he was Canadian because of the uniform, but he was pretty sick from a head wound and couldn't tell them anything."

"Imagine stealing from a wounded man!" Mama exclaimed.

"They shipped him to London, but they didn't know who he was for certain until the fever left him," Tommy said. "Knowing he's coming home is the best Christmas present we could ever have."

Meredith caught sight of a solider lugging his kit bag toward Port Stuart's small hotel, an empty sleeve pinned to his shoulder. Endings weren't always happy, but better a lost arm than a lost life. The war had changed some things forever, even here in Port Stuart.

Meredith's toes were beginning to freeze and the tips of her fingers were nipped by the cold despite the smart new gloves. She quickened her pace, eager to reach home.

A brilliant red cardinal on a branch beside the boardwalk cocked its head at her as if to ask, "Any more news?"

How would she ever keep her secret until Christmas Day?

✚✚✚

"Tommy should take her upstairs," Mama whispered as she and Meredith sat with their tea at the kitchen table once the supper dishes were done. Bernadette was curled up with the five kittens in a tangle beside her, all of them fast asleep on the braided rug in front of the hearth. Firelight danced along the walls, and the red-and-white curtains at the kitchen window shut out the night sky. Tommy and Ellen were playing snakes-and-ladders at the other end of the table, whoops of glee alternating with moans of despair.

"She's worn out, poor lamb, and no wonder." Mama reached for the big brown teapot and filled her cup. "We'll fatten her up while she's here. Tommy, too. As a matter of fact," she continued, eyeing Meredith, "I'm beginning to think they don't believe in feeding young people in Toronto."

"Mrs. Butters thought you'd say that," Meredith said. "She told me to tell you that fattening me up will be her New Year's resolution."

"Mrs. Butters sounds like a sensible woman. I just hope they aren't working you too hard." Mama pushed a plate of shortbread across the table. "You'd better have another cookie before Ellen finishes them off."

Meredith had been turning her news over and over in her mind since her conversation with Dr. Waterton last night. She'd wanted to tell Tommy today on the train, but Mama deserved to hear it first.

"Can I have one?" Ellen climbed into Mama's lap and reached for the plate of cookies. "Tommy, too?"

"Of course," Mama said as she wrapped her arms around Ellen. "Cookies are for eating."

"Merry's not eating hers."

How Meredith had missed Ellen's wicked little grin!

"She was wool-gathering on the train, too," Tommy said, moving to the chair beside Meredith and reaching for a cookie.

"Were there sheep on the train?" Ellen frowned.

"It means not paying attention to what's going on around you," said Mama. "I've noticed it, too. I think it might be something to do with Christmas."

Meredith made up her mind. "It was going to be a Christmas present, but I want to tell you my news now."

"News isn't a present!" Ellen exclaimed.

"Of course it is," Tommy said, tugging on one of Ellen's braids, "if it's good news like the news about my brother."

Ellen screwed up her face in reply.

"I think it's good news, and I hope you'll think so, too." Meredith stole a glance at Tommy. "Last night there was a Christmas party in the kitchen at Glenwaring."

"Mrs. Butters and Forrest and Bernie and me," Tommy said, "and Meredith, of course."

They'd been sitting around the kitchen table, talking and laughing, sharing the turkey dinner Meredith had helped prepare. Mrs. Butters had made a little speech in memory of Parker, her face rosy from the heat, and they'd all sat silent for a few moments.

Just that week, a letter from Parker's mother in England had set the household buzzing. They'd learned that Parker had been sending money to England regularly to support a wife and daughter.

"Who'd have thought?" Forrest had said at the time. "Imagine Parker with a wife and daughter!"

Parker had guarded his privacy so strictly that Meredith wondered if he'd been afraid of something, and whether it was loneliness for his family that made him so difficult. She liked to think she'd have been nicer to Parker if she'd understood more about him, but that was something she'd never know now.

"God rest his soul," Forrest had said at last, after Mrs. Butters' speech last night. They'd all echoed him solemnly, and then Forrest had proposed an outrageous toast to Bernie that made everyone laugh.

"Merry!" Ellen bounced on her mother's lap. "You're wool-gathering again!"

"We all received presents from the Watertons," Meredith said quickly. "You know about my coat, but there was a bicycle for Tommy and a doll for Bernie. And we had gifts for each other, too."

"It was grand," Tommy said, nodding.

Meredith had been on tenterhooks while Tommy

unwrapped the woolen mittens Mrs. Butters had helped her knit for him. His pleased grin warmed her right through, but she'd been speechless when she opened his gift to her.

"I know you like to read," Tommy had said as she lifted a slim book of poetry from its wrapping. As she turned it over, the gold letters on the cover caught the light: *The Watchman and Other Poems*, by Lucy Maud Montgomery. "I hope you like it," he'd added quietly.

"It was perfect," Meredith said now, her fingers caressing the leather cover of the book in her pocket. "Then, after the party," she went on, "Dr. Waterton called me into the library."

✚✚✚

The doctor had looked so serious she thought he must have bad news, but Aunt Jane was supposed to be getting better. Had something happened to Mama? Or Ellen?

"I've been doing some digging, Miss Hollings," the doctor had said from behind the big desk, "and I've discovered that you're too young to be working at a job like this."

Of all the unlikely things he could have said, that was the unlikeliest. Meredith had felt a chill despite the cozy fire in the hearth. How had he found out? No one in Toronto knew her real age.

"If we'd known you were only thirteen, we would

never have agreed to hire you, as I told Mrs. Stinson yesterday." Dr. Waterton looked at Meredith over the top of his glasses.

"I'm sorry," Meredith whispered. He must have already asked Mrs. Stinson to find someone to take her place. She was going to be sent away just as that horrible woman had predicted.

"But if we hadn't hired you," the doctor continued, "then we wouldn't be in your debt."

Startled, Meredith had looked up to see Dr. Waterton smiling broadly. "This household came through the flu epidemic due, in large part, to you, Miss Hollings," the doctor said. "You are a remarkable young woman."

That was the second most unlikely thing he'd said. "Thank you, sir."

"Thoroughly remarkable, as I told your mother when I wrote to tell her how much we are in your debt," the doctor said. "She wrote back telling me that you left school to take this job, and she told me why. She also told me you'd planned to become a teacher."

Meredith nodded, but there wasn't any point thinking about something that was years and years away.

"I have asked Mrs. Stinson to engage someone so that Mrs. Butters will have help during the day—"

She was being let go after all! How would she ever tell Mama?

"—so you can finish school here in Toronto."

"I—I don't understand, sir."

"It's simple." Maggie stood in the doorway, holding out a brand new copybook and pen tied with a bright red ribbon.

Meredith looked from Maggie to the doctor.

"You'll continue to work here with Mrs. Butters in the morning and the evening," Dr. Waterton said, "but starting in January you'll be free to attend school during the day."

"I can work? And go to school at the same time?" This was more than she could ever have hoped for.

"I don't think that will be a problem for a remarkable young woman like you," Dr. Waterton said.

"A copybook isn't much of a Christmas present, in my opinion," Maggie handed the slate to Meredith, "but I have a feeling it's just what you wanted."

✚✚✚

During Meredith's story, the fire had burned down to embers that cast a rosy light on Bernie and the kittens. Meredith nibbled at the shortbread cookie, savoring its buttery-sugary deliciousness.

"Such a nice man." Mama sighed. "I never expected this. It's the answer to my prayers."

"I'd like to have Merry for my teacher," Ellen said,

yawning, "when she's finished working in Toronto."

"She might want to teach in Toronto, you know." Tommy reached across the table and tweaked Ellen's nose. "She might not want to come back here."

"I'll always come back here," Meredith said. "I missed you so much, Mama, and you, Ellen," she reached for their hands, "and I missed this house, the way it fits me exactly."

"Maybe one day Toronto might fit you, too?" Tommy asked quietly.

Meredith remembered the grinning boy from the shoeshine stand who'd rescued her stockings. "Maybe," Meredith said. "One day." She couldn't help grinning herself.

HISTORICAL NOTE ON *YESTERDAY'S DEAD*

In the late summer of 1918, the 500,000 citizens of Toronto, Ontario, were weary from four long years of war. Many young servicemen and women had died overseas. Everyone hoped that the peace talks in Europe would end the war at last.

Few people in Toronto suspected that they would soon be fighting a fearsome enemy at home. Newspapers had begun to report on a new illness that struck healthy young adults suddenly and killed rapidly.

The new killer was named the "Spanish Flu" because people thought it had started in Spain. Historians now believe this form of influenza first appeared in the mid-western United States in the spring of 1918. It quieted over the summer, but in August a new, more deadly form appeared on a military base near Boston, Massachusetts. It spread to Europe as troopships delivered American soldiers to the war. It quickly infected the tired, undernourished soldiers fighting in the trenches, and then spread around the world.

Before it died out in 1919, the Spanish Flu killed an estimated 30,000 to 50,000 people across Canada, and 50 million to 100 million people worldwide. Historians estimate that one in every forty people who caught the Spanish Flu died from it. If a similar outbreak occurred now, estimates are that between 110,000 and 190,000 Canadians would die.

Influenza viruses are crafty survivors. They mutate easily into new forms and find new ways to infect people. Influenza causes aches and severe tiredness, and the mucus that builds up in the lungs can cause pneumonia. Before antibiotics were invented, severe pneumonia usually killed its sufferers. Even today, between 4,000 and 8,000 Canadians die each year as a result of influenza.

The Spanish Flu was different from "regular" seasonal influenza. Once infected with the virus, people became sick very rapidly, and the resulting pneumonia was particularly dangerous. Some accounts tell of people who died within twenty-four hours of showing the first symptom.

Toronto newspapers reported on the high numbers of

sick and dying in cities such as Boston and Montreal, but medical personnel and city officials couldn't agree about whether the Spanish Flu would reach Toronto. When it did arrive, it was at first confined to the nearby army camps and to the city's military hospital. But once it entered the general population, it spread like wildfire. On October 2, 1918, the newspapers reported the second death from the Spanish Flu. By October 8, just six days later, Toronto hospitals were full and city workers were preparing two abandoned hotels to serve as hospitals. The Spanish Flu or its associated pneumonia caused seventy-two deaths on Friday, October 11 alone. By Friday, October 18, the total number of confirmed deaths in Toronto had reached 392; one week later, it had climbed to 1,023.

Confusion contributed to the high number of deaths, since many people who were sick did not seek medical attention because they thought they just had an ordinary cold or the regular seasonal flu. Historians believe that many deaths from the Spanish Flu went unconfirmed.

Symptoms varied, too. The Spanish Flu generally began with sudden weakness, pain, chills, headache, and fever. Delirium was common. Sufferers coughed up quantities of bloodstained mucus. The tongue could become dry and brown. A bloody froth might come from the nose and mouth. The pneumonia could turn faces and fingers blue, a sign that the lungs were not getting enough oxygen.

2

"FLU" DEATH RATE UP, MORE VICTIMS TO-DAY

Crowded Hospitals and Heavy Demand for Aid Is the Report.

392 DEATHS IN CITY SINCE FLU OUTBREAK

Twenty-Seven More Succumbed to Malady in Toronto To-day.

Deaths Registered, City Hall.

	Influenza.	Pneu.
Oct. 1-17..	239	126
Oct. 18 (to noon),. ...	16	11
Total deaths... ...	255	137
Total deaths... ...		392
Total deaths, same disease, same period of 1917		18

THE FLU DEATH TOLL 1,023 SINCE OCT. 1

Fourteen Deaths Were Registered at City Hall Before 11 A.M. To-day.

DEATH REGISTRATIONS, CITY HALL.

	Influ.	Pneu.
October 1-25..................	691	318
October 26 (to noon).....	11	3
Total.....	702	321
Grand Total..........		1,023
Total for same period, 1917....		27
Increase...		996

Deaths From All Causes.

October 1-20...	773
Monday...	145
Tuesday...	140
Wednesday.............	.81
Thursday..	113
Friday...........	113
Saturday (to noon)....	20

Forty-Six Nurses at General are Sick Out of Staff of 211.

CAN'T TAKE PATIENTS

Western Hospital Is Avoiding Operation Cases So as to Nurse the Influenza.

A FIFTH OF LONDON CITIZENS HAVE "FLU"

12,000 Cases in City—503 Soldiers Ill—Schools, Churches, and Amusements Closed.

London, Ont., Oct. 15.—According to the estimate of physi-

MANY "FLU" VICTIMS

Thirty-Five Deaths Registered At City Hall Since Noon Yesterday.

Influenza has claimed 19 more vic-

A collection of headlines from *The Toronto Daily Star* from October 1918

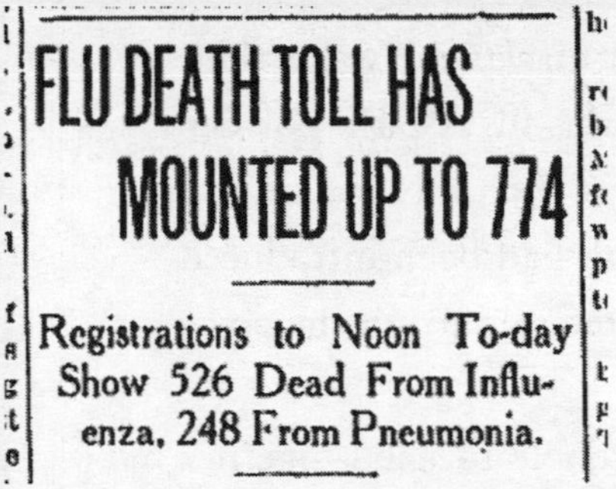

FLU DEATH TOLL HAS MOUNTED UP TO 774

Registrations to Noon To-day Show 526 Dead From Influenza, 248 From Pneumonia.

For about six weeks, the Spanish Flu affected every aspect of life in Toronto. Schools and churches were closed. Bowling alleys, billiard rooms, dance halls, and theaters were shut. No library books were circulated. The telephone company asked people to use the telephone only in emergencies because so many operators were ill themselves or nursing family members at home.

Wage earners in Toronto faced a difficult choice: should they go to work and risk catching the Spanish Flu, or stay home and lose wages? Those caring for the sick faced a more agonizing choice: help the sick and possibly bring the illness home to their own families, or keep away. Retired doctors were asked to help and women were urged to take basic nursing courses. Volunteers from churches and community groups prepared food in soup kitchens set up to help feed families stricken by the Spanish Flu.

It wasn't clear how you could avoid getting sick. Doctors didn't know whether people who had the Spanish Flu could infect others before they showed any symptoms. They advised staying away from infected persons and crowded places where you might be exposed to the airborne germs thought to cause the disease.

People were told to wear a mask and wash their hands if caring for someone who was ill. Aspirin powder, the only modern remedy available at the time, was helpful to bring down fever. (The pill form had been introduced during the war, but many people preferred to stir the powder into water.)

"Folk" remedies abounded. People mashed together such things as mustard, onions and hot lard, and then wrapped the mixture in a cloth and applied this "poultice" to the throat or chest. Others believed that drinking coffee mixed with mustard, or warm milk mixed with ginger, sugar, salt and pepper, would kill any germs! Goose grease, garlic, oil of cinnamon, and toxic ingredients such as camphor, sulfur, turpentine, carbolic acid and creosote (a black, tarry substance) were all rumored to be helpful.

Makers of patent medicines—medicines sold in drugstores without a doctor's prescription—claimed that their products could prevent or treat the Spanish Flu. Many of these medicines contained toxic ingredients like those listed above. They were often sold door to door or advertised in the newspaper, sometimes on the same pages where public health authorities warned readers against using them.

A typical ad from *The Toronto Daily Star* in October 1918 for Dr. Chase's Menthol Bag, manufactured by Edmanson, Bates and Company Ltd. in Toronto, reads:

These bags are pinned on the chest outside of the underwear, and the heat from the body causes the menthol fumes to rise and mingle with the air you breathe, thereby killing the germs and protecting you against Spanish Influenza and all infectious diseases.

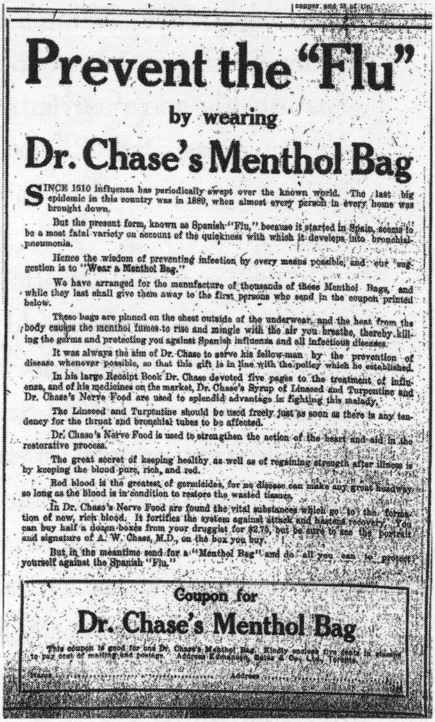

Dr. Chase's Menthol Bag
ad from 1918

Imagine being surrounded by people who stank of menthol (a mixture made from peppermint or other mint oils), mothballs, turpentine, garlic, onions, and tar!

The Spanish Flu generally struck adults between the ages of 18 and 45. However, the epidemic drastically affected many children in Toronto. In families where one or both parents were sick, children could go hungry because there was no one to prepare food, or no money to buy more. Coal deliveries were suspended because the drivers were ill, so many houses went unheated as winter approached. Many children became orphans. Often children needed care because their mother had died from the Spanish Flu and their father was serving in the armed forces overseas. The Children's Aid Society and the public health nurses worked hard to meet the needs of these children.

The Spanish Flu continued well into 1919 in Canada and other parts of the world. In fact, the epidemic halted hockey's 1919 Stanley Cup series at two wins each for the Montreal Canadians and Seattle Mariners, making 1919 the only year that the Cup was not awarded.

The custom of the time called for a black sash to be hung on the door of a house where someone had recently died. Black sashes on hundreds of Toronto doors served as grim evidence of the power of the dreadful disease. In all, more than 1,700 Torontonians died from the Spanish Influenza.

AUTHOR'S NOTE

Meredith's story is made up of many different aspects of life in Toronto in 1918. The Waterton family was lucky to have a household staff. The occupations open to young women were growing—nurses, clerks, telephone operators, sales staff and, of course, teachers. As a result, jobs as domestic servants in Canada declined steadily after World War I.

Shea's Palace was a popular vaudeville theater on Yonge Street, but I invented Galligan's, the grocery store on Yonge Street that Meredith and Tommy visit. It would have been similar to Higgins and Burke, a successful store there at the time.

In 1918, *Mrs. Beeton's Book of Household Management* was a respected source of information on cooking and housekeeping even though it was written in 1861! A cook like Mrs. Butters could well have had it in her kitchen. It's available online.

The airplane industry was just beginning during World War I. The war offered an opportunity to use this new technology. The book on airplanes that Jack browsed was written by John B. Rathburn and published in 1918.

The 1916 book of poetry by Lucy Maud Montgomery that Tommy gave to Meredith was a wonderful find.

Air Marshall William Avery Bishop—Billy Bishop—was Canada's number one air hero from World War I. He flew patrols with his squadron of planes and conducted solo flights behind enemy lines, winning 72 "dog fights"—battles in the air—in 1917 and 1918. For an entertaining look at his extraordinary life, you can visit www.billybishop.net.

ACKNOWLEDGMENTS

Toronto's history is filled with terrific stories. The City of Toronto, through the Toronto Arts Council, generously provided financial support during the writing of this one. I would like to thank Second Story Press and editor Jonathan Schmidt, who saw the potential in Meredith's story and worked with me to bring out the best in it.

Karen Krossing, Patricia McCowan, Karen Rankin and Sarah Raymond provided unflagging support, astute observations, and wise advice over many cups of tea. Peter Carver and many participants in his Writing for Children workshops rooted for Meredith and provided insightful feedback.

My children, Kathleen and Harrison, and my husband Barry, cheered me on word by word, chapter by chapter. Their love and support made traveling the long road to a first novel easier.

ABOUT THE AUTHOR

PAT BOURKE is a freelance business writer and editor whose previous careers included strategy consultant and high school math teacher. She is a member of the Board of Directors of the Tippet Foundation, a charitable foundation that funds not-for-profit arts, education, and community organizations primarily in the Greater Toronto Area. She lives in Toronto with her husband, and children. Visit her at www.patbourke.com.